EDNA AND GENEVIEVE ESCAPE FROM CURMUDGEON AVENUE

(Curmudgeon Avenue Book Three)

Samantha Henthorn

©Samantha Henthorn, 2019.

All rights reserved. This book or any portion thereof
may not be reproduced or used in any manner whatsoever
without the express written permission of the publisher
except for the use of brief quotations in a book review.

This is a work of fiction. Names, characters, places, businesses, incidents or events are either the product of the author's imagination or used in a fictitious manner.

Any resemblance to any place or person living or dead is purely coincidental.

This book was written with British English spelling and grammar, including a northern turn-of-phrase. No one ever says 'and I' in Manchester.

 A Readers' Favorite five star book.

This book is dedicated to the reader, especially those who have never been to Todmorden.

CHAPTER 1: BREAD, TWICE A DAY.

When we return to Curmudgeon Avenue for the third time, the wind had blown in the truth about the tall, handsome stranger with the well fancy car. Harold and Edith had been relieved to discover that he is neither an elephant detective nor a fraud investigator, and Toonan was disappointed he was not interested in her either. The tall, handsome stranger turned out to be Matteo Dubois, looking for his mother, Genevieve Dubois.

And although Matteo did not find Genevieve on Curmudgeon Avenue, you have probably guessed that he is about to cause a disturbance; FINALLY! There is hope that the set of nincompoops that live here currently will move out and leave me in peace! Edna had already escaped with Genevieve, which was a real shame for me because Edna was one of the less annoying ones...

....

The sun shone through the dirty curtains of the holiday gite Edna and Genevieve had landed in the previous evening. Particles of dust danced through the air – even dirt was romantic today. To Edna Payne, an ex's return had never been as good as this. Never as heart-thumpingly rewarding as Genevieve appearing underneath Curmudgeon Avenue's bedroom window.

Genevieve was already up and about of course; Edna could smell the black coffee wafting up the wooden staircase. It would be coffee and croissants this morning, and every morning from now on. No more burnt toast, no more disagreeable nephew, no more stupid sister, and absolutely no chance of bumping into that imbecile Harold... Edna had escaped! Edna and Genevieve had escaped! And Edna was not the only one who could not believe her luck.

'Bonjour!' Genevieve sang at the bedroom door. She had already been out to the boulangerie - French people buy bread twice a day, everyone knows that.

'What time is it?' Edna ran her dry tongue across her teeth.

'Oh, it is just before noon, you must have needed your sleep after our long, loong journey,' Genevieve elongated.

'Oh, I'm still tired, come back to bed, Genevieve,' Edna patted the bed beside her and dust billowed up into the room like a smokescreen. 'Oh,' Coughed Edna, dampening the mood. 'Why couldn't we have stayed in that hotel a bit longer?'

'Non!' Genevieve tutted. 'This was not an l'hotel it was a stop-gap, a tourist convenience, you said you wanted us to live in France, this *is* France, my love, bread twice a day and life in a gite.' Genevieve knelt on the eiderdown and cheekily stole a corner of Edna's baked item. Edna's face contorted into a picture of culpability. Had she really wanted this?

'Well, at least the weather is nice, no need for an umbrella here,' said Edna as she opened the window. Living the French life is starting to suit her after all. 'What are we going to do today?' Edna began to fuss about with her suitcase. Which turtle-neck jumper was she going to wear today?

'Do?' asked Genevieve.

'Yes, what are we going to do?'

'Nothing! That's the beauty of it, it is nearly noon, almost time for my afternoon nap, everything is shut in the early afternoon.'

'Everything?' said Edna.

'Oui, everything!'

'But there isn't *anything*... Never mind *everything* around here,' exasperated Edna.

The two women made their way into the garden and claimed a rusty garden lounger each. Genevieve continued her rationales and benefits of doing nothing. Including wisdom that as long as there was bread twice a day, plus cheese and wine on offer, they would want for nothing more. Edna drifted back off to sleep, it was reading that caused it. As she lay there with the French sun caressing her eyelids, Edna dreamt of painting impressions of her life; or how life was about to be, in France. Her colour palette narrowed as she illustrated peasant's food in her sleep. Still, the brushstrokes were broad and adventurous as the apples in her dreams morphed into other kinds of foods, grapes, bananas, blueberries, strawberries, all kinds of fruit. Roast lamb, cured ham, battered spam; chips, chops and onion gravy, fish supper, takeaway Indian, stone-baked pizza. Even Bury Black Puddings made an appearance, their round, black shapes darkening Edna's dream. Tea, cups of tea! Hot chocolate swirling around in a big mug, clouds of lemonade bursting bubbles on her face. What's this?! Edna got up with a start. 'It's raining! It's raining, Genevieve! Get up!' Edna shook Madame Dubois awake.

'Sacre bleu!' Genevieve grabbed her fancy

throw and bundled herself and Edna inside the gite.

'The weather is just as unpredictable here in Brittany as it is in… Britain!' Edna laughed.

'It is just a shower, Edna, do not worry.'

The two women sat at the window watching the rain until they realised that it really was not *'just a shower'*. Electrical storms lit up the sky and robbed the adventurous couple of their power. As the sun went down, candles were lit.

'Do not worry, Edna, we have bread and cheese,' said Genevieve. Edna's thoughts turned to the several large plastic canisters filled with gallons of wine she had spied on her way up the stairs… Edna and Genevieve played 'I spy' they played 'forehead detective' they had a bit of a cuddle. Still, Edna's mind was fixed on drowning her sorrows along with her French dreams.

'Let's have a tipple, Genevieve,' Edna said.

'Tres-Bien!' agreed Genevieve. Edna made a dash for it to the kitchen to retrieve two wine glasses. She hastily gave them a quick rinse and shine. T*he alcohol will kill any bugs* Edna said to herself (and to no one else, Edna would never let herself appear dirty in public). Genevieve then dragged the gallons of wine up the stairs.

'Help me, Edna! You are stronger than I,' Genevieve Frenched it up for Edna's benefit, and it worked. Edna shoved Genevieve upstairs towards the dusty bedroom, already drunk on excitement.

'I'd better grab another couple of wines, just in case,' Edna said, and as her feet landed on the ground floor, they became damp with rain… Dirty rainwater had seeped in through the crack under the gite's front door, and in through the flimsy veranda that decorated each French window. Edna grabbed a couple of receptacles to catch the drips. This was futile, as the floor was already nearly covered.

'We have a flood!' Edna sang as she bounded upstairs to Genevieve, who had already poured two glasses of red wine, her face illuminated by candle-light.

'Ah! My love! We have escaped, and now we are imprisoned!' Genevieve said. 'Cheers!' The two women clinked their glasses together in harmony, their eyes transfixed on one another.

'This reminds me of when I moved back to Curmudgeon Avenue, Edith and I had to take in lodgers so that we could afford the luxury roof… I'm not doing that again!' Edna used her wine glass to illustrate her point. 'We could always move back there!'

'Where?' Genevieve's face shrank into a picture of uncertainty.

'Curmudgeon Avenue… I'm only joking, Genevieve, I just meant that I've sorted out one roof, I'm not sorting out another!' Edna's face twitched with anxiety. Forgetting that Genevieve is a flight risk, she didn't want to lose her again.

'Oh, hahaha!' Genevieve did her best fake laugh. 'Come on, Edna, drink your wine. It's only a shower, and I don't want to return to Cuuuuurmudgeon Avinoo,' she curled her French accent around my name as though she was unable to pronounce it correctly.

I knew, but little did Edna know that Madame Genevieve Dubois was never, ever able to return to Curmudgeon Avenue, or any part of Whitefield, England, ever again. Not even if she wanted to…

CHAPTER 2: THE NEW NEIGHBOUR.

'Hello darling,' Mrs Ali looked up from her word search puzzle book to greet the man who is furthest from anyone's darling in Whitefield at the moment, Ricky Ricketts.

'Alright Mrs Ali, you got any of those mint chocolate thins left that you had on sale that time?'

'No, and never mind that!' she batted Ricky on the arm with her puzzle book. 'What about the new neighbour?'

'New neighbour?'

'Yes, Mr Dubois, the one Harold thought, was chasing him! Turns out he was looking for...'

'I know that bit! I mean what do *you* mean, new neighbour?' Ricky very rudely interrupted Mrs Ali.

'Ah, he has bought Number Three! The house that he lived in with his mother all those years ago!' said Mrs Ali.

'No way!'

'Yes, way!'

'Blimey, that house has been empty for ages, eww, I wouldn't want to live there I bet it's well minging.' Ricky bared his brown teeth as he spoke, gifting Mrs Ali with his own minging death breath.

'Rumour has it he's renovating it to open a business,' Mrs Ali absentmindedly circled the word *rival* in her word search puzzle.

'Oh yeah? What sort of business?' Don't forget, Ricky only came into the shop to buy some *After Eight Mints.* Mrs Ali's eyes scoured her shop, they were alone, and so she jumped off her little stool and popped the 'closed' sign on the door.

'He's opening a shop!'

'Shit!'

'I know!'

'What are you going to do?' said Ricky.

'Nothing! Everyone knows that this is the most popular shop in Whitefield,' Mrs Ali wrapped her shawl around her torso. Ricky said nothing. 'I will just carry on providing a good service best shop in Whitefield. If Mr Dubois wants to ride on my coattails, then let him.'

'I think it was easier when we thought he was a fraud investigator,' said Ricky, helping himself to some penny chews.

'Oh, how *is* Toonan after her disappointment?' Mrs Ali batted away Ricky's thieving hands. 'I know she wanted him to be her stalker, but I think we all knew that was wishful thinking.'

'I know, she's stupid. Wouldn't like it if someone actually was stalking her!' Ricky said. (Hark at him, coming over all responsible!) 'How gutted was she though?' Ricky laughed, (that's more like it, you horrible little twerp).

'Oh dear, poor Toonan, unlucky in love,' said Mrs Ali.

'Never mind her, 'poor Ricky' you want to be saying.'

'Why? What's happened now?'

(Need you ask Mrs Ali? Wantha has obviously dumped Ricky Ricketts again).

'Women troubles,' Ricky said, shaking his head as though he really did have troubles.

'Ha! Women plural?' Mrs Ali asked. Just then, the front door of the shop rattled. The silhouette of a tall, smartly dressed, handsome man could be seen amongst Mrs Ali's advertisement cards that hang in the glass door. 'Oh! It's him! It's Mr Dubois!' Mrs Ali clutched Ricky's forearm. They both instinctively grabbed handfuls of penny chews, popping them in their mouths to relieve their anxiety. The front door rattled again, proving the popularity of the most popular shop in Whitefield.

'Hello!' Matteo Dubois shouted. 'You are usually open at this time!'

'Quick, let him in, Ricky!' Mrs Ali said 'I can't let him think that I am not open for business, ready for anything in the most popular shop in Whitefield!' Mrs Ali barely managed to finish her sentence, before Matteo was in the shop, selecting essential items for himself. Milk, today's newspaper and a chocolate bar. Ricky silently observed, watching his every move while popping penny chews in his mouth, one by one. Matteo did not flinch. He was almost a foot taller than Ricky Ricketts and had no reason to return any hostility.

'Thank you,' he said to Mrs Ali.

'Thank you, darling,' she said. Ricky raised an eyebrow at her, realising that everyone was Mrs Ali's darling. 'Do you need anything else?' she asked, the shop almost echoing with its newly found silence.

'No, that's everything for today, thank you.' Mr Dubois silently made his way back to the door but turned in afterthought towards Mrs Ali. 'Oh, I meant to say, I hear there is a rumour that I'm opening a shop?'

Mrs Ali and Ricky Ricketts gasped in union,

Ricky almost choked on his pilfered goods.

'Still no word on your mother then?' Mrs Ali deflected.

'No,' he said in his indecipherable accent. 'I still do not know who my mother really is.' Matteo Dubois swung the shop door behind him, leaving his ambiguous sentence hanging in the air like burnt chillies.

'That reminds me,' said Mrs Ali. 'I'd better check on that curry paste I'm making!' she sashayed backwards into her private quarters. Not only did she have a potential rival for her shop, but she also had a contender for her title of twice as nice yet twice as nosy. Here was Matteo Dubois, polite, pleasant, yet he seemed to know about the gossip...

'Who started that rumour then?' Ricky was well confused.

'Shh! Ricky, I'm thinking,' Mrs Ali returned from the back with a balled fist nestled into her forehead. 'He didn't actually answer me, did he?'

'Well you didn't give him a chance, did you?' Ricky was back on the penny chews. 'Does that mean you started the rumour yourself?'

'What! No... You were about to tell me that you have women troubles... Women plural!'

'Oh, it's a long story,' Ricky shifted and looked at his feet as though he had just realised he had stood in dog dirt.

'Well, was it just chocolates you wanted?' Mrs Ali 'Just the one box? Only I won't be selling you anti-freeze at the same time, I don't want to be appearing on *Crimewatch*!'

'Just the one box and I owe you for all those penny chews,' said Ricky.

'Don't worry darling, you'll be sending me your dentist bills!' Mrs Ali smiled a smile that did not meet her eyes because her eyes had met with Ricky's teeth again.

'Ha! Well I'm going round me mum's now, her and Harold have been hiding under the kitchen table. Now I know why, they're hiding from their new neighbour!'

....

Back at Matteo's residence on Curmudgeon Avenue, he sucked on his cigarette with redundant anticipation. Everyone on this Whitefield street seemed familiar with his 'mother'. Foreign to Whitefield culture he failed to realise Mrs Ali was just doing what Whitefield folk do, familiarity breeds friendships.

Flicking through childhood photo albums, the ones that used to make him feel safe, Matteo now saw their truth. The boy, Matteo dressed up in countless different school uniforms because of all the house moves they made. Genevieve always pretended that this was because *'Matteo just couldn't settle'*, but now he knew that it was not him. It was her, Genevieve Dubois, moving from her life just as people got too close; too close to discover the truth. Genevieve Dubois, the young woman, reflecting out of those childhood photos standing behind Matteo like a mannequin. Young, beautiful, too young to have a son Matteo's age, surely?

Photos of Matteo as a teenager. Again, Genevieve still looking too young to be his adopted mother. Then into his twenties, the photos included snaps of Matteo with evidence of cash in hand employment, paint splattered across his *Joe Bloggs* long-sleeved top (remember those?). Or what about the Italian pizza sauce spilt on his *'On the seventh day, God created Manchester'* T-shirt? Matteo had sought a Mancunian identity during his meaningless existence.

On those photographs, another woman had started to appear like a creeping Jesus. Tall, big-boned, nose in the air, wearing a turtle neck jumper. Of course, I am talking about Edna Payne. His sense of abandonment was ripe and angry, as, during his adult years, Matteo had not been able to maintain a steady relationship. If Genevieve was not here, then where was she? Who was she? And more importantly, who was Matteo Dubois?

One thing was certain to Matteo, whoever *he* was; Genevieve Dubois is a big fat liar.

CHAPTER 3: MEANWHILE, EN FRANCE.

After several attempts at translation and several hours of trying to bail out rain from the gite's ground floor, Genevieve realised that her choice of sanctuary for Edna and herself was an unsuitable hovel.

'His accent is very thick,' Genevieve hid her mouth and whispered to Edna. The holiday gite's landlord was making charade type movements to indicate that the drowned pair should have escaped in a boat. 'Bateau,' he was saying as he laughed a hearty laugh.

'He is saying we should have had a bath!' Genevieve wrongly said. 'I think he means you, mon amie,' Genevieve nudged Edna and winked at the landlord, who frowned in confusion.

'Same to you, Genevieve, neither of us has attended to our personal hygiene for days!' Edna shrivelled into her turtle neck jumper. She was correct; Edna and Genevieve had been trapped in the upstairs rooms of the gite for almost a week. The rainwater gradually subsided, and the landlord appeared on the scene when it was almost too late. They had nothing but wine, cheese, stale bread, and each other to survive on since the flood. Cabin fever at boiling point, the two of them continued to free the gite of the remaining rainwater, the landlord disappeared in the confusion that his help was too late.

'Well, I think that's the last of it,' Genevieve brushed the mud out of the house, and opened the front door for the first time in days. Then the two women spilt out onto the front garden like a popped champagne cork. The sun shone on the lush green landscape, birds sang, along with the sing-song voice of the neighbouring farming wife.

'Bonjour!' she said to Edna's delight and Genevieve's fear. As luck would have it, she knew enough English to save them from further floods. 'Je m'apelle Adele, enchantee, I have some milk and eggs for sale if you need anything?'

'Oh! Oui,' Edna said. 'Oh, Genevieve, you do the talking.'

''Ow did you cope with zee flood?' Causing further amusement and confusion, Genevieve spoke in English, but with an exaggerated French accent.

'What flood?' Adele said.

'Well, my goodness, we have been cooped up in the upstairs rooms for days because of the rainwater!' Edna's smile faded as she accepted the bread that Adele passed to her from her basket.

'Oh, I'm soo sorry, we just presumed you were either out, or erm… enjoying each other's company!' she winked. Adele, a pretty young woman, was not to blame for Edna, and Genevieve's imprisonment yet felt somehow responsible (Edna has that effect on people). 'I think that the gite has flooded before, but only if it rains as it did, the farmhouse is immune to this kind of disaster, my 'usband makes sure the pipes are free of obstruction.' Adele took in more of the scene and smells that the two women presented her with.

'Do you mean that this flood could have been avoided?' Genevieve spoke in English again.

'Oui just needs some work to clear any obstructions… could even be flies.'

'Flies?' the two women replied.

'Dead flies, oui, all French buildings have flies, I thought you would know sis?' Adele raised an eyebrow at Genevieve.

'Not enough to cause a flood!' Genevieve said, (nice save!)

'Oh, I told you last night, Genevieve, I don't want to be sorting out any more leaky buildings.'

'Hmm, then you told me you wanted to move

back to Curmudgeon Avenoo!' Genevieve narrowed her eyes. Adele looked from one woman to the other, all she had offered was the basics, now she was getting into a mild case of a domestic. Edna regretted her words immediately; she did not want to lose Genevieve again.

'Well,' Adele said, avoiding her milk souring to cream. 'A nice couple who we sell produce to own a chateau that they rent holiday rooms out.'

'Oh, and are they French?' Edna said, all excited.

'Non, Ecossais.'

'Oh, well they sound perfect, I think we might be on the move again, Edna!' Genevieve decided for both of them. Fortunately, Edna was only too pleased.

'First, allow me to lend you the use of my bathroom then we will make them a telephone call,' Adele sorted everything out, like only French farmers know how.

Edna and Genevieve raced each other to the bathroom, Genevieve winning of course. When she returned, Edna was in the middle of a facetime call on Adele's laptop with Diane and Jackson.

'Oh, here she is!' said Edna.

'Enchantee,' Jackson said from behind the

screen. 'We've just been arranging for you and your fancy piece to move into our home!'

'Oh!' said Genevieve, clutching the towel around her head, as though all her problems had been solved.

'You can help us brush up on our French!' said Diane.

Genevieve's towel turban collapsed in a mess of wet hair and despair around her shoulders.

CHAPTER 4: HAROLD AND EDITH DECIDE IT IS BEST TO HIDE FROM MATTEO.

'Is he still there, do you think?' Harold and Edith had been hiding under the kitchen table for longer than was reasonably necessary. The sound of the back door opening widened both their eyes, and Edith dug her fingernails into Harold's forearm.

'What are you two doing under the table? I just told Mrs Ali I thought that's where you'd be, but I was joking!' Ricky Ricketts dragged one of the foldaway kitchen chairs out from under the table, and Harold and Edith slowly emerged from their hiding place with creaky dismay.

'Oh, it's been terrible since our new neighbour moved in, Son!' Edith said, smoothing down her pleated skirt.

'Terrible,' Harold nodded his wobbly head.

'Why, what's he done?'

Harold and Edith went on to recount events of the days since Matteo Dubois revealed his true identity, breaking Toonan's heart and Harold's pride in one go. All Matteo did was admit that his mother is Genevieve Dubois, it was not his fault. Matteo did not ask to be born... or adopted. Having returned to Curmudgeon Avenue, he was, quite rightly dismayed that the fools living at Number One had taken over part of his garden. His efforts to rattle the large brass door knocker on their front door had been in vain. So he did the next best thing, traditional in places such as Whitefield, as Edith explained to Ricky Ricketts.

'I was minding my own business, pegging out the washing, and he popped his head over the back garden wall,' Edith's eyes fluttered in disgust. 'I don't know where he thought he was? Radcliffe probably!'

Harold shuffled in his foldaway chair, being a former Radcliffe resident himself.

'Anyway, he asked me to chop down the climbing creepers.'

'What?' said Ricky.

'The climbing plants... he asked me to cut them down!' said Edith.

'Why?'

'Apparently, they have grown over into his back garden, but how was I to know? I haven't been looking into his back garden, have I?' Edith spoke with the blazing eyes of modern suburban problems. 'Not like him, he's been having a good look,' she finished by folding her arms in petty annoyance.

'I know, you could have been topless sunbathing or something, hey Harold!' Ricky winked at Harold, who attempted a laddish type guffaw.

'It's very unsettling,' Edith went on (this could take a while…) 'Then, there was the issue with the wheelie bins.'

'Not the wheelie bins!' Ricky said, helping himself to a scotch egg while Harold shuffled backwards out of the kitchen. Like many Borough of Bury residents, Edith is obsessed with her wheelie bins. There is a complicated system whereby different types of recycling get collected from different coloured bins every three weeks on rotation. The bins, of course, are mostly donated to each household by the local council, but ownership is key - Whitefield folk do not like sharing their rubbish, but Matteo was obviously not aware of this unspoken rule, as Edith explained;

'So, we returned from the weekly shop on bin day, and blow me if our driveway was empty! I knew straight away who had taken our bins; it was as though he couldn't see our number '1' painted on the side. The bin cleaner said it happens a lot, people who don't pay for their bins to be cleaned often steal the clean ones so that they can have three weeks of luxury!' Edith had not stopped talking for quite some time, but she hadn't finished yet. 'We got them back, of course. Harold waited for the all-clear and then opened his gate and got them back.'

'Problem solved then!' said Ricky, 'It was probably a misunderstanding.'

But the problem was not solved, not in Edith's view. She had a restless night's sleep when the back garden security lights danced on her duvet. She could hear someone rolling her wheelie bins around in her back yard, she was sure of it. Edith lay there, awake, thinking up plans and booby traps to catch the bin thief, until sleep caught up with her and delivered her to the following morning. But the damage was done, Edith had taken a disliking to her new neighbour, and Matteo Dubois had done nothing (not really) to deserve it.

Mrs Ali, despite her proud assertions of the best shop in Whitefield, did not want a rival.

Edith wanted her bins, climbing creepers and no neighbours.

Harold had advised Edith that it was best to hide from Matteo after Harold told him that they knew nothing of the whereabouts of Madame Genevieve Dubois (as you know, there is a long and convoluted lie here).

Ricky just wanted a quiet life, as we recently found out, he has women troubles. That's women plural, more about that later… Did you notice that Wantha and Toonan are not visiting Curmudgeon Avenue with him? No - they are safely tucked up in their mother's house on the Hillock estate.

CHAPTER 5: 'IT IS FORBIDDEN!'

Edna and Genevieve were on the road again, driving on the right-hand side on the expanse of flat landscape and into south-west France.

'Oh, look! That sign says it is the way to the Dordogne region, I would love to go there!' Edna waved her hand with an air of fake sophistication, which Genevieve put an end to by screwing her nose up and shaking her head.

'It is revolting,' Genevieve turned towards the window. Steady on, Edna and Genevieve! You cannot both have your noses in the air at the same time; at least one of you should keep your eye on this lonely road, which was garnished with grapevines.

'Well, I've heard it is a beautiful part of France,' Edna said.

'Onwards, Edna, onwards to the south of Bordeaux...' Genevieve was at it now, using her hands to direct the conversation, like all good liars know how.

The two women were silent for longer than was reasonably necessary. Tarmac and the Ford Cortina engine making that soothing driving sound. Both of them lost in their own thoughts…

Edna recalled the first time she had heard a French accent. It belonged to Genevieve of course. Smoking at the front of Curmudgeon Avenue, extinguishing the cigarette in the little metal grille attached to the front wall of Number Three (it's not there now, by the way). Genevieve had spotted Edna bumbling down the street in her polyester caftan. Edna had been waiting to speak to her sophisticated, French neighbour for quite some time. She planned this would improve her social standing… well; Edna got more than she bargained for that day didn't she! There was something about the way that Genevieve spoke; a French accent in Whitefield in the 1980s would have been the very height of sophistication. Even now, it had not lost its charm. Genevieve could get away with anything with that voice… Speaking of which, Genevieve was also in a world of her own, remembering a snapshot of her own past…

A school coach trip, accompanied by the rowdy shouting and singing of teenagers as so often they are. It all got a bit too much for one handsome, olive-skinned young male with a stylish floppy fringe. He stood at the front, swept his hair out of his eyes and shouted: '*It is forbidden!*' in his gorgeous French accent. Genevieve was convinced that his gentle, hazel eyes had fixed on hers... Finally! She had been trying to attract his attention for days. Genevieve sang even louder due to his request, 'It is forbidden'. The rest of the school coach laughed even more deafeningly than any singing or shouting could produce. While the boy's companion explained that the word 'forbidden' may not be the appropriate adjective in this sentence.

Confused as to why a beautiful French male on a school coach full of Catholic school children would be a novelty? Madame Genevieve Dubois was not confused. It was almost as if she was born that day, everyone deserves a bit of fun... even if it is forbidden.

It was mid-afternoon when Edna and Genevieve arrived at Château Le Grincheaux. As you know, mid-afternoon means that everything in France is closed, not so here. The two women were met by two smiling red faces belonging to Mr and Mrs Bove, Diane and Jackson. Have you ever heard a Scottish person speaking French? Well, Edna and Genevieve were about to as Diane greeted them, paying particular attention to Genevieve, grabbing her by her upper arms with both hands. Genevieve turned her head away in the same fashion as a French person about to *La Bise*.

'Oh, it's your accent, Diane, leave the poor woman alone, they've had a long drive!' said Jackson, to the rescue.

'Hello, I'm Edna,' she shook Jackson's hand, surprising him with her manly grip.

Well, the mid-afternoon came alive into the early evening, with food, wine and good company. The Boves were a laid back sort of people, happy to accept Edna and Genevieve as their temporary guests on the say-so that they could stay longer if they liked it there. Edna said that she would make that decision after the next rainfall, (which made her sound like some sort of witch, but no one questioned this). The more Genevieve drank, the dodgier her accent became, skating between broad Lancastrian to what could pass as a character in the British situation comedy *'Allo 'Allo!* No one noticed, Diane and Jackson are a fun couple, living the dream in their sunshine castle.

'Whereabouts are you originally from, Genevieve?' Diane asked.

'Oh, all around France, yooo know…' Genevieve waved her hands in the air attempting to impress sobriety.

'Paris, isn't it?' Edna said, squeezing Genevieve's knee fondly. 'I remember when we first met, I thought you were so sophisticated, a Parisian in Whitefield.'

'Paris it is then,' smiled Genevieve, picking up Edna's hand and kissing it. 'Whitefield is in North Manchester,' she deflected.

'Oh, they most likely know that, Genevieve… who cares about Whitefield!' Edna laughed away the awkward tinge in the air.

As night turned into the early hours of the following day, it was time to wrap up the soiree. Edna stuck her nose in the air with promises of checking the ceiling for leaks, and Genevieve batted her long eyelashes. Mr and Mrs Bove climbed into their luxury four-poster bed, both slightly tipsy, but able to hold their drink (a lot) better than their two new light-weight guests.

'There's more to those two than meets the eye!' said Diane.

'That there is, wifey, that there is!' said Jackson.

'Och, you always take a shine to the female guests!'

'I thought that's what you meant about more than meets the eye! Did you shake that Edna's hand? Very manly,' said Jackson, his eyes now starting to droop.

'No, oh my goodness! Oh! Do you think that's

why she was wearing that turtleneck jumper? You know, to hide her Adam's apple?'

'Aye, she was, wasn't she? Well hang on, what did you mean then, if it wasn't her manly grip?'

'Oh, the other one, she didn't speak a word of French, and her accent slipped into something off *Coronation Street* after a few wines.'

'Oh haha well, they're paying guests, and I'm sure we'll get to know them in the fullness of time.'

That you will, Mr and Mrs Bove that you will…

CHAPTER 6: EVER WONDERED WHY SOFT CHEESE IS SO POPULAR IN FRANCE?

The following morning at the Chateau Le Grincheaux, Mr Jackson Bove was the first to wake and start his day. He had slept well, and his mind benefitted from some overnight restoration. The first thing he thought of when he awoke was that one of the new female guests looked familiar. As he was getting dressed, Jackson decided that he had been distracted by Edna's mysterious and manly handshake. As he tiptoed downstairs (so as not to wake Mrs Bove), he changed his mind... Surely if Genevieve were to be recognised, then he would have known her straight away - not on the following day?

But as Jackson Bove opened the door, letting in the daylight and commencing his morning bread journey, he changed his mind back again. There *was* something oh so familiar about the French woman.

You know what it's like when you're watching a film, and you vaguely recognise one of the actors, but cannot place them? Your mind wanders until you remember where you had seen them before (or you can look on IMDB – I've seen Ricky Ricketts do it when he was watching a BBC drama). Well, that is how Jackson was feeling about Genevieve, very distracted. Only he could not look her up on the internet. Walking around the little market, Jackson made a conscious effort to keep his mind on the task at hand. Bread, milk and eggs were bought. Then it was on to the cheese section. A soft brie, a Port Salut, and for Mrs Bove, a hard cheddar (a particular favourite of hers but not as popular in France as the soft cheeses).

What reason did Mr Bove have to get in Mrs Bove's good books?

Well, I have it on good authority that Jackson suggested spying on the female couple in their room. There is a print of the painting *Madame de Pompadour at Her Tambour Frame,* inherited from the chateau's previous owners. During the renovation, they discovered that holes had been created in the painting's eyes, concealing further holes in the wall. And an integrated set of tunnels and mirrors allowed the person on the other side of that wall to see into the guest bedroom...

Jackson and Diane decided to keep this cheeky detail as some sort of curio, a quirk of their Chateau. They vowed never to spy on any of their guests, and even fashioned a false cupboard door which hung on the other-side of the wall hiding the spy-hole. In theory, it could be unlocked and utilised by Mr and Mrs Bove, should they need to. Not until this moment, after a few years of opening up their home to guests had the spy hole ever come up in conversation...

Hence the cheese...

'You animal!' Mrs Bove had said before falling asleep the previous night. Initially, she said this in a jokey way, following their light-hearted conversation about Edna's man hands. But Mr Bove would not let the subject drop.

'I'm not a perv, I just want to know who I've really got under my roof! It's a man's right!'

This is where the conversation turned sour. It was the word 'perv' that did it...

Mr Bove was now back at the chateau, part one of his mission accomplished (favourite cheese bought), yet still, no nearer to finding out about the female guests. Maybe his wife had managed to get something out of them while he had been out shopping?

'Ah, Bonjour Monsieur!' Edna giggled. 'Comment Ca Va?'

'Very well, thank you, Edna,' Jackson answered.

'Bonjour,' sing songed Genevieve 'Will you join us for a coffee?'

'Oh, yes thank you,' Jackson suspiciously eyed the builder size mug Genevieve had selected for him, don't the French like an espresso? Hmm, maybe she was unable to find the small cups? Or perhaps she presumed I liked a mug because I'm Scottish? *Careful not to read too much into things,* Jackson thought.

'Mr Bove?' Genevieve was standing right in front of him.

'Oh! Thank you, sorry I must've drifted off!'

The three of them sat down at the solid oak table in the morning room, looking out of the window, taking in the beautiful expanse of the French countryside.

'Oh, I'll get some plates out for our breakfast. I take it you like bread and cheese?' Jackson said. (Well, yes they do, Jackson, if not getting a little sick of it. Edna's digestive system is not enjoying the extra gas). 'Only I saw this hard cheddar for sale, its Mrs Bove's favourite! Where is she though?'

'Oh, we haven't seen Mrs Bove, we came downstairs and thought you must be together?' Edna said.

'Oh, no, I was cautious not to wake her when I got up; I crept out of the house and have just been to the little market.' Jackson got up, it was very unusual for his wife to have a lie-in, she was a real morning person. He made his way to the staircase, about to check on his wife when he could hear her making her way downstairs. 'Oh, hello, sleepyhead!' he said.

'I know! I don't think I've ever slept in so long, oh my goodness!' Diane said, her face all baggy from either not enough, or too much sleep.

'Bonjour, Diane!' Edna and Genevieve chorused with smiles. 'Come and join us, I expect you need a coffee?' Edna's voice as refined as she could make it.

'Aye, and none of your little French espresso cups! Give me a big mug today, please! And three sugars!'

'Oh, three sugars!' Edna tittered. 'Reminds me of my nephew.'

'A wee laddie drinking coffee?' said Diane.

'Oh, no, he's almost forty years old now, haha!'

And so the chit-chat ensued. Mrs Bove started to come round after her lie in. Jackson fussed around with the bread and soft cheese, which Edna and Genevieve appreciated. Gifting the hard cheddar to his wife had the desired effect that the Bove's 'perv' argument had been forgotten about.

'Oh, my head! I feel hung-over! I don't know what's up with me!' Diane eyed her husband and could not resist the joke that popped into her head. 'Oh, you're not slowly drugging me, are you, husband? Like that woman did to her fella in Rocamadour?'

Before Jackson had the chance to deny such a travesty, Genevieve let out a short sharp cough. 'Oh, pardon, I think a bit of bread just went down the wrong hole! Oh, Pardon,' Genevieve repeated but had not managed to dissuade Diane's train of thought; she was chuckling away at the misfortune of the tale.

'Yes, you won't have heard the news in Manchester, or the north, or wherever you were. I think it might have been about this time last year; this woman from the Dordogne region poisoned her husband with sleeping pills. Nothing suspicious at first, but I think they looked into it, and two of her other ex-lovers had died in suspicious circumstances,' said Diane.

'No! Ha, well, I've only one wife, and what's the point in bumping you off, Diane? You've no life insurance! That's why she did it, they reckon, for the insurance money,' said Jackson.

'Oh, my goodness, no, that news did not reach us in the UK. I presume this woman is safely behind bars now?' Edna said as Genevieve quietly nibbled a corner of hard cheddar.

'No, she went on the run, and I think I'm right; they never caught her. Is that what happened, Jackson?'

'I think so, Diane; I don't remember seeing anything on the news about her since they were calling her the Black Widow of Rocamadour. She could still be there, hiding in plain sight.'

'Well, that's a shame, I would love to visit Rocamadour, if only for its name!' said Edna.

Genevieve started coughing again. Coughing, spluttering and choking on her hard cheese.

CHAPTER 7: RUMBLINGS.

Meanwhile, in Curmudgeon Avenue... Matteo's mind was full of ambition.

For all we know, he too, could have been dreaming about cheese. We just don't know. One thing is for sure, Matteo dreamt of working for himself. From small beginnings, he envisaged great things. Ironically beautiful that Number Three Curmudgeon Avenue should become available on the property market just as he was looking for a location for his small beginnings.

Matteo could not fail...

And when Francesca saw his success, she would surely come back to him; it was not too late. A somewhat convoluted and elaborate plan for a business venture, but Matteo had been planning this, planning and dreaming. Quick Matteo! Stop daydreaming! Firstly, he had a renovation project to complete and could not do this alone.

The front door tinkled in Mrs Ali's shop. (Don't worry, Matteo's not about to ask her for help with manual labour, not directly).

'Hello, I need to place an advertisement in your shop window, how much is it?'

(Not that old chestnut again?)

'Oh, oh, special rate for you, darling! We business people need to stick together, don't we?' Mrs Ali then proceeded to charge double the going rate for one of her shop window advertisement spaces.

'We do, Mrs Ali, I have a good feeling about this street,' Matteo went on to write out his advert:

'Wanted, Builders, Tradesmen required for a renovation project, good rates of pay, enquiries to Number Three, Curmudgeon Avenue.'

'What line of business did you say you were in again?' Mrs Ali, usually skilled with her natural sense of nosiness, forced a nonchalant smile in Matteo's direction.

'I didn't,' smirked Matteo. Oh, he was going to have some fun with Mrs Ali! But Mrs Ali had her own set of cards to play. When the coast was clear, she made her way to the front of the most popular shop in Whitefield and peeled Matteo's advert out of its little see-through sleeve.

'This can go straight into Ricky Ricketts' hands. I'm sure he'll be needing the work more than anyone now!' Mrs Ali said to herself. She rearranged the other advertisement cards to make it look as though they had not been tampered with, should Matteo Dubois glance at the shop front on his way past. Reassuring herself that doing a good turn for Ricky Ricketts at this precise moment was a *very* good turn. The universe may even reward her for her kindness to him, even if it would be at Matteo's expense.

Meanwhile, at Lidl supermarket, Harold and Edith were busily filling their shopping trolley (and occasionally, Harold's rucksack) with their weekly goods. Harold was running out of baby wipes (don't ask), and Edith, skilled in the role of wife, had remembered.

Ahh, I am rather enjoying this picture of domestic bliss, even if it is Harold and Edith. Gemma Hampsons' mother was operating the till that Harold and Edith selected today. She recognised them immediately, but Edith was struggling to place her.

'Hello, love,' she said, in a rather excited manner for a supermarket till operative.

'Oh, hello!' Edith said, hurriedly ladling all her shopping onto the conveyer belt while desperately trying to remember where she knew this woman from. She scanned the packet of baby wipes through the checkout and held them up in both corners.

'Getting ready, are we?' Mrs Hampsons chuckled.

'Do you mind?' Harold snatched his baby wipes out of Mrs Hampsons' hands and threw them into the empty trolley.

'Don't mind him,' Edith rolled her eyes at Harold for Mrs Hampsons' benefit, clueless as to what she had been referring to with the baby wipes. Mrs Hampsons was one till beep away from revealing that Mr Hampsons had been a bit grumpy when he found out… But decided against it, as the checkout rigmarole had ended for Harold and Edith.

'And there's your receipt. I expect we'll be seeing more of you in a few months then…' Mrs Hampsons grinned and watched Harold and Edith exit the shop.

'We won't be seeing more of the inside of Lidl if that's what the staff are like! The cheek of it! Getting ready? If a man can't utilise the soft, moist comfort of a baby wipe in the privacy of his own bathroom, then I don't know what the world is coming to!' Harold's head wobbled.

'Harold, I've told you before, you need to see a doctor about your bowel habits… I knew that woman on the till from somewhere. I can't think where but I think she was talking to me about the baby wipes.' Edith rolled one of her front teeth across her bottom lip, freeing a tiny bit of dead skin in thought.

'Nonsense, Edith! Why would she be talking to you!' said Harold… (I hate him).

The legendary duo turned the corner of Curmudgeon Avenue in their purple Morris Marina. 'Oh, I'm so thirsty for a cup of tea, Harold.' Edith said, her mind wandering to mundane tasks such as putting away the frozen shopping first and then putting the kettle on… when it dawned on her that she had forgotten to buy milk!

'Oh, blast, we forgot to get milk, Harold. I'll have to pop to Mrs Ali's,' Edith's dreams of a rewarding cup of tea after the draining weekly shop were disappearing. She would have to put all of the shopping away, and then there would be some other distraction inside the big house that needed a lot of housework. It's a wonder that Edith doesn't become dehydrated! But what's this? Harold is about to become helpful and considerate towards his wife?!

'I'll go, Edith, you start putting the shopping away, and I'll go to Mrs Ali's.'

'Oh, Harold!' said the easily pleased Edith as she lugged the extra heavy bag for life shopping bags into the house.

'Morning, Mrs Ali,' Harold said as he entered the corner shop. 'Edith forgot to put milk in the shopping trolley, so I thought I'd do her a favour and come and buy some milk from you.' Harold tutted and rolled his eyes and pulled a milk carton from the fridge.

'Oh, hello darling, oh, doing Edith a favour? Don't you drink tea yourself anymore?'

Harold ignored Mrs Ali's meaning, while painstakingly counting out the small change in copper and silver coins, he gestured towards the magazine display.

'I don't want Edith reading any more of these stupid women's magazines... They fill her head with nonsense and give her ideas about what to moan and nag me about!' Harold could be rather forthright when he wanted to, but don't worry, Mrs Ali does not suffer fools gladly.

'Oh, darling! I can't imagine Edith having anything to moan about now that she's married to you!'

(I honestly don't know how this woman keeps a straight face).

'Exactly!' Harold's eyes widened with enthusiasm and agreement with everyone's favourite life guru, Mrs Ali. 'Some people are not happy unless they have something to moan about!'

'Oh, I know Harold, some people do like moaning,' Mrs Ali smiled. Harold turned to leave. Mrs Ali's shop had served a purpose for Harold today, having saved him from the mild peril of Edith's magazine obsession. So it was only fair that Mrs Ali called in a favour from Harold. The best way to do this is without his knowledge. 'Oh, Harold, before you go, I've noticed that Ricky has not called around to Curmudgeon Avenue for a few days…'

'Have you?'

'Yes, he was here three days ago when Mr Dubois popped in. I've had another little chat with Mr Dubois since – as a matter of fact, it's your new neighbour that I needed to speak to Ricky about.'

'I shouldn't worry; Ricky will turn up when he runs out of food or money. Ha! He's probably round there now; what shall I tell him?'

'It's this advert that Mr Dubois has put in my window.' Mrs Ali took the little card out from her till.

'It's not in your window now, is it?'

'No, I saved it for Ricky… after all; he'll be needing the money in a few months, won't he?'

Harold raised an eyebrow and read the card, 'Good rates of pay, hmm?'

'Harold!'

'You must give this card to Ricky Ricketts. I would love for him to be inside Number Three, doing the renovation work.'

'Okaaay...'

'Yes, oh, and make sure when he applies for the job, he tells Mr Dubois that he saw the advert in my window – very important.'

'In your window, OK, Mrs Ali, see you soon!'

When Harold returned home, he could see Edith sitting at the kitchen table, and to his horror, she had a magazine in her hands. 'Where have you been? You've been ages. I've managed to put all the shopping away all by myself!' Edith shrieked.

'What on earth is that?' Harold said, all goggle-eyed, pointing at the magazine.

'Oh, when you were reading the instructions on that jar of pickles for ages, I noticed they've started selling magazines at the supermarket now!' Edith had treated herself.

'Right well, no reading quizzes about how to improve your sex life, please!' Harold frowned and rubbed his lower back while dropping teabags into mugs. 'Oh, I've got this for your Ricky.'

'Hmm, he's not been around for days,' said Edith reading the job advert card. 'Well, he's not usually in the job market, and it says, tradesmen. Mind you, I'm sure he could do a bit of decorating if he put his mind to it.'

'Mrs Ali seemed rather keen that he gets this job, and he has to pretend he saw the card in her window.'

'She'll have charged Mr Dubois for the advert,' Edith slurped the cup of tea Harold had just made.

'Not only that, but she also said that Ricky will need the money in a few months!' Harold's eyebrows were narrating their own story now on his forehead. Edith looked up at him and sucked in a lot of air all at once.

'OH! That's the second time someone has said something like that to us today! What's happening in a few months then?'

CHAPTER 8: EDNA BECOMES FIXATED WITH ROCAMADOUR.

Edna slid her feet around on the white Egyptian cotton sheets' comfortable and clean feeling. Genevieve lay naked next to her, under the duvet which lifted and fell gently with every breath she took. The sweet sun trespassed gently into their bedroom through the blinds. Edna had never been so happy in all her life, here in a French castle, becoming rather fond of these afternoon naps. Far away from Whitefield, with the love of her life... Madame Genevieve Dubois turned over to face Edna executing a massively explosive cough, the phlegm of which landed in Edna's face.

'EWW!' Edna bolted up and grabbed a tissue from the box at the side of her bed.

'Oh, pardon, mon amie, my love,' Genevieve

coughed and spluttered her rib cage rattling with catarrh as she fussed around Edna. There was much whooping, coughing and laughter here.

'Oh, hahaha ohhh,' Edna changed her tune. 'You just gave me a shock hahaha,' nervously… 'Oh, you didn't do it on purpose, are you ok, Genevieve?'

'Oui, oh desole Edna,' Genevieve said, rubbing her chest. 'A smoker's cough, I think,' she flopped back into bed and sighed.

'What if you've got a chest infection? Are you feeling hot?' Edna held the back of her hand across Genevieve's forehead. 'Hmm, I don't know, but maybe you should visit a doctor.'

'Oh, non! No, Edna, it is just a smoker's cough!'

'Well, maybe you should give up then. You were feeling a little hot, I think…' Edna came over all concerned for Genevieve.

'I am hot. I'm hot for you, Ednaaaa!' This exchange created more laughing and shrieking.

In the bedroom down the hall, chateau owners Diane and Jackson's afternoon relaxation time was disturbed. Jackson was looking at the newspaper, and Diane read a lengthy historical novel about Eleanor of Aquitaine by Elizabeth Chadwick.

'Och have you heard those two at it again,'

Diane whispered to Jackson. 'I can hardly hear myself think, I'm never going to get into this novel.'

'Aye, do you think we should say something?'

'NO, no, we'll just maybe go and sit downstairs or something if it carries on. They're on holiday after all.'

Diane and Jackson resumed their reading in silence. After a few moments, the booming sound of Edna's laugh could be heard echoing down the integrated set of tunnels and mirrors that formed the spy hole between the guest bedroom and the landing. The chateau owners looked at one another and released their respective reading matters from their hands.

'There's nothing else for it,' said Diane.

'Do you mean you're thinking what I'm thinking?' said Jackson.

'I am,' nodded Diane, putting her book under her arm.

'Right, you fetch the key for the secret cupboard, and I'll check that the coast is clear. Our guests are still making a lot of noise.'

'NO! You ejit! I meant we should go downstairs for our chill-out time, let these two love birds have a bit of privacy!' Diane left the room, muttering to herself about blocking up the spy hole.

....

Late afternoon arrived, bringing with it Edna bounding down the stairs in a caftan, costume jewellery jangling around her neck and wrists like a wind chime in your neighbour's garden.

'Bonsoir, Diane!' Edna said.

'Oh, hello, Edna, oh we were just wondering where you two were, weren't we, Jackson?'

'Aye!' said the embarrassed male who could not look Edna in the eye after what he thought he heard earlier.

'Genevieve is still resting upstairs, she's got a bit of a cough. Hmm, I think she should go to the doctor. She says it's a smoker's cough,' Edna flopped down on to the wicker conservatory chair, Diane winced. Jackson arrived with some whiskeys and ice in tumblers.

'What's that you're reading, Diane? Oh, I love reading!' said Edna, snatching the novel out of Diane's hands. 'Oh, a historical fiction? Eleanor of Aquitaine?'

'Yes,' Diane cast an eye over Edna's fingers thumbing the pages of her new book. 'I've been meaning to read it for a while, and when we were talking about Rocamadour the other day, it reminded me and jumped straight to the top of my reading list,' Diane sang as she took the book from Edna.

'Oh, is that where it's set?'

'Well...' Diane started, but Edna interrupted...

'Tell me more about this Rocamadour place. It's got a great name. Roc-am-a-doooooour!' Edna would not let Diane get a word in (and she thinks it is only Edith that does that). She jangled her costume jewellery as though she suited it. Diane raised one eyebrow at Edna; she was renting her a room in her home, not providing the entertainment.

'Well, I've never been to be truthful, but I would like to. It's a famous sacred place, a place of pilgrimages,' Diane noticed Edna opening her mouth to speak, so she held her heavy novel up in the air. 'That's why I wanted to read these novels about Eleanor of Aquitaine. She stayed there in medieval times, and apparently, it's hardly changed. Let's get it up on the internet; I don't think that it would be too much of a drive for you and Genevieve to get to it if you wanted to while you're here.'

The two women started looking at websites designed to help people plan their day trips. For a small village, Rocamadour attracts plenty of tourists.

'Bonsoir,' an exhausted Genevieve entered the scene. 'What's this we're on now?' she coughed and wearily sat down near Edna.

'Oh, Genevieve,' Edna crowded her lover. 'I have just been finding out about that place, Rocamadour!'

As Edna spoke with exuberance, Genevieve's face contorted into a portrait of a person watching a horror movie.

'Look at this, the medieval buildings are clinging to the side of this cliff!'

'A steeeep cliff,' Genevieve nodded.

'There are lots of steps for the tourists to climb up to the - oh look at this Genevieve, the quaint little street with beautiful cafes and interesting shops!'

'Fppp! Over two hundred steps, Edna and they have been there 1000 years, for pilgrims, not tourists,' Genevieve dismissed.

'Pilgrims? Tourists? Same thing if you think about it!' Edna enthused. 'It has a sacred Black Madonna in one of the churches. I wonder if you can see it?'

'Oh, Edna, there are plenty of those around France; think of St Sara in the south! Lourdes, there are loads of sacred places. Pah!' Genevieve gestured to Diane, who was edging her way out of the room.

'Oh, there is even a monkey forest nearby!' Edna clapped her hands together.

'I'm going for a smoke, Edna.' Genevieve stuck

an upright cigarette in Edna's face. She slumped without grace to the terrace, where she met Jackson, watering the roses.

'Hello there,' Jackson said, busy in the garden. Genevieve nodded and sucked in her cigarette as though the thing was giving her life. Each inhale slowly turned wheezy Genevieve into glamorous Madame Dubois. With one final cough and spit, she sat upright in her garden chair, expertly took pins out of her hair; one split second later, it was a smooth and stylish French chignon. She wiped yesterday's eye makeup from underneath her eyes, drew on a slick of red lipstick without even looking in a mirror and firmly placed her large sunglasses on her face. It was then that Genevieve realised she was being watched. From behind another pair of sunglasses and an extensive historical novel sat Diane, shaded on the other side of the terrace. Diane's lips pulsed with amusement; the sound of phlegm escaping had alerted her. Genevieve let out a little token of surprise, and her posture grew with each realisation that someone's eyes were on her. Before a conversation could start between the two women, Edna flung open the French doors, both arms of her caftan displayed like a pair of wings.

'OH, we definitely need to go to Rocamadour!' Edna sang, her nostrils flaring with announcement. 'I have just found out that it has a population of only SIX HUNDRED people!' Edna grinned from ear to ear; it did not suit her.

'Aye, that'll be five hundred and ninety-eight people now that woman bumped off her husband and ran away!' said Jackson, having heard Edna's loud proclamation. The owners of the neighbouring chateau one hundred miles away probably heard her too. Genevieve shrunk back into her lounger and quietly coughed.

CHAPTER 9: THE LESSER SPOTTED WANTHA ROSE.

On this particular day in Curmudgeon Avenue, Harold had a hankering for a peach. A ripe, round juicy, soft fruit. Edith thought she was being taken out on a date, but Harold was just thinking of himself, so they were out and about again for a Bury town centre trip. With its *World Famous Market*, tasty food venues and expansive shopping centre. Bury really had become local enough to Curmudgeon Avenue for Harold and Edith to go out on a date *because that's what married people do*. Edith had read all about it in one of her forbidden women's magazines, date days for married people (not necessarily to Bury town centre). Unfortunately for Edith, Harold was in a bad mood (what did you expect, Edith?)

'Those people came in fifteen minutes after us and were served first in that cafe!' Harold's head wobbled about like one half of a deely-bopper.

'Never mind, Harold...' Edith deflated. 'Oh, look! Sale on at Marks and Spencer!' she dragged Harold by the hand to the department store. Harold rolled his eyebrows.

'I'm going to the food hall, you go and look at women's cardigans, and I'll meet you at the lift in fifteen minutes!' Harold ordered, patting his wrist-watch with his forefinger.

Edith made her way up to the women's department in the elevator. She didn't even want a cardigan. Harold could be so bossy sometimes. She started looking at the clothes, patterned floral items first, of course. Edith looked in the mirror, holding a rose coloured jumper dress up to her figure. There was no point going to the changing room if the colour didn't suit her. As she admired her own reflection during the fifteen minutes of freedom that Harold had allowed her, something caught Edith's eye in the mirror. Behind her was a glimpse of some very distinctive and recognisable glorious, yellow afro hair. Edith turned around like a shot... She was sure that Wantha was behind her, rooting through the underwear section, but now she was nowhere to be seen. Edith started darting about the clothes rails, still no sight of her son's girlfriend. Come to think of it, Wantha had not visited Curmudgeon Avenue for three or four weeks. And Ricky Ricketts himself had not called for a few days. They could not have fallen out again, because Ricky would be back sleeping on the settee downstairs. Edith continued to search, and oh dear! Her fifteen minutes might be up!

'Wantha! Wantha!' Edith shouted near the escalators. Initially, no one answered her. 'Wantha! Wantha!'

'Are you alright, madam?' A shop assistant approached Edith.

'Oh, yes, sorry, I thought I saw my son's girlfriend, well I think she's his girlfriend, only I haven't seen either of them recently, and now I can't find her and..'

The shop assistant gathered that this could go on for quite some time and eyed up the rose coloured item Edith was clutching. 'Well, I'm sure you'll find her eventually. Would you like to use our changing rooms before you go downstairs?'

'Oh!' Edith said, also noticing she was still clutching the jumper dress. 'Oh, no need, I held it up against myself in the mirror.'

'Ah, good idea, well I suppose it doesn't matter too much what nightwear looks like, as long as it fits,' the shop assistant said. 'And keeps you warm; these thermal nightdresses are excellent quality this year.'

Nightdress? Edith thought to herself, looking at what she thought was a jumper dress. She shoved the coat hanger into the shop assistant's bemused hands and made a dash for it down the escalator. Edith was sure her fifteen minutes had ended, and Harold would be waiting for her.

Edith saw the person she was really looking for on the opposite upward incline, making her way back upstairs. Another customer stood directly in front of her, obscuring Edith's view. It was definitely Wantha. No one else in the Bury area had that hair-do. Despite Edith's attention-grabbing shouts of her name, Wantha sailed right past Edith without even looking at her.

Meanwhile, over by the lifts (the correct meeting place), Harold had been waiting for Edith for longer than was reasonably necessary. He had purchased a box of what he felt was overpriced muesli and a *tin* of peaches - they would have to do. Where is Edith? She has most likely been unable to choose herself a new cardigan. Harold grumbled, sniffed, swallowed, and looked at his wristwatch for the sixty-fifth time. His foot was tapping, his manner inpatient. He tried to ring Edith on her mobile phone, but it rang out (on the table inside Number One Curmudgeon Avenue). Oh, I'd better go and look for her; this is a flaming nuisance. He pressed the 'up' button on the lift doors and tapped his foot impatiently for it to come down.

'Finally!' The steel lift doors opened to reveal the sight of someone Harold had not seen for three or four weeks. Spilling out of the lift was a very pregnant looking Wantha... A fellow customer angrily caught Harold's open-mouthed expression.

'Oi! Are you getting in this lift or not?'

Harold was now upstairs, and Edith was downstairs, waiting for Harold. Oh, maybe I should have brought my mobile with me? (Yes, you should, Edith, because Harold has rung you again, and it is making an awful rattling vibration on the table). Edith decided to go back upstairs. She might have got it wrong; Harold may have meant meet at the TOP of the escalator. Edith thought she saw Wantha again ahead of her. She shouted her name, but it turned out to be a child wearing a fluffy yellow jumper on her father's shoulders (very dangerous on an escalator). Then, on the opposite downwards escalator, she noticed Harold.

'There you are!' Edith shouted, but it was as though she hadn't. Harold also sailed right past Edith, got to the bottom and made his way back to the lifts; maybe Edith would be there by now. But as you know, she wasn't. Edith dashed past the original shop assistant and jumped on the downwards escalator, expecting to see Harold waiting patiently at the bottom...

'Oh, for goodness, sakes! HAROLD!' Edith started shouting, and over by the lifts, Harold recognised the nagging shriek of his wife. Eventually, the happy couple located one another and exchanged blame.

'You said the escalator.'

'I said the lifts, and why didn't you answer your mobile?'

'I didn't bring it out; I didn't think I'd be making any calls to anyone on our romantic date in Bury town centre!'

This line of bickering continued until Harold and Edith were back at the car park. Harold made a joke out of asking Edith for the car keys and then pulled them out of his jacket pocket. This resulted in silence until it was absolutely necessary to speak again.

'Oh Harold, I forgot to tell you, I saw Wantha!... I saw Wantha, and she ignored me!'

'Oh, blimey!' An open-mouthed, driving Harold said. 'I saw her too! Did you notice her surprise?'

'No, what surprise?'

'PREGNANT Edith, unmistakeably pregnant! I think we know why Ricky hasn't been visiting...'

CHAPTER 10: THERE MUST BE SOMETHING IN THE WATER AT CURMUDGEON AVENUE.

When Harold and Edith turned the purple Morris Marina into Curmudgeon Avenue, the inside of the car was full of anticipatory grandparent chatter. Harold was undecided if he should and would be referred to as 'Grandad Goatshed'. Edith had already and excitedly chosen 'Nanna Edith,' on account (very thoughtfully) towards the other grandmother, that 'Grandma Patchouli,' had a nice ring to it. They did not notice Mrs Ali standing outside her shop, swilling out dirty water from a mop bucket, her mouth making a little 'O' shape when she saw Harold and Edith.

'Oh, Harold… I've just thought, that's what the till operator at Lidl must've meant when she said we were getting ready, with those baby wipes. But how did she know?'

'Wantha probably shops at Lidl,' Harold said. As they opened and closed the up and over garage door at the back of Curmudgeon Avenue, their new neighbour popped his head over the back wall.

'Congratulations!' he nodded. The pair of them giggled nervously.

'Liberty,' whispered Edith under her breath.

'We don't need congratulating for having adequate parking facilities in our own home…' Harold whispered, and Edith agreed. They opened the back door. Harold was looking forward to eating an entire tin of peaches all to himself. They were met by the sombre looking image of Ricky Ricketts, and beside him sat an overexcited blooming female, who neither Edith nor Harold recognised.

'Oh, hello,' Edith reached the seated Ricky to give him a greeting hug, noticing that his general odour was much improved compared to normal.

'Hello Mum,' Ricky said, nodding at Harold. The blooming female half stood, only to be given a subtle hint on the forearm that Ricky was to do the talking today. 'This is Gemma, my new girlfriend.'

Harold and Edith both stared at Gemma and then at each other.

'Ah ha ha,' Gemma gave way to flirtatious familiarity. 'Oh, we've known each other years Ricky! I'm not *new,* not really.'

'Right, well yeah erm,' Ricky awkwardly squeaked in his leather jacket. 'Where have you been?'

'We've been out shopping, Richard,' Harold said. 'Where have you been? I mean, it's not to say that I've missed you coming round here for your post - where is his post, Edith? But your mother might like to hear from you.' Harold wobbled his head and slipped his arm around Edith's waist.

'Oh, don't worry, I've made him change his postal address to my house,' Gemma spoke with a reassuring yet slightly patronising '*I'll sort Ricky out, don't worry'* tone.

'Well, Mrs Ali has missed you too,' said Edith. 'She gave Harold a bit of paper for you. What was it again? Tell him to look in Mrs Ali's window?'

'What?' said Harold, releasing Edith from his grope. 'Oh yes, no, it was a job advert... Next door needs a bit of renovating doing, which is very good of her to think of you for the job opportunity. You have to say that you saw the card in Mrs Ali's window, I think she's charging him.'

'All sorted,' said Ricky. 'That bloke who you thought was a fraud investigator has bought the house next door.'

'Yes, we know that bit!' said Harold.

'Did you know he wants to open a shop, though? He's hired me to help with the building renovations. And I've put him in touch with my guy over the electrics.' Ricky came over the 'big I am', resulting in Gemma fluttering her eyelashes at him.

'The liberty!' Edith said. 'Well, what about Mrs Ali's shop? The most popular shop in Whitefield?'

'Nothing like a bit of competition,' said Ricky.

'Oh blazes, that means that folk will be walking up and down Curmudgeon Avenue, comparing the prices and looking through our front window,' Harold spoke as though he has lived here all his life.

'It did use to be a shop years ago, I can't remember what, but there was a duplex flat upstairs… Wait, what kind of shop is it?' said Edith.

'Well, that's the thing,' said Ricky, with both sweaty palms on the Formica. 'He's asked me to sign a disclaimer, swearing me to secrecy about what line of business it's going to be.'

This admission instantly interested Harold. His face broke into a knowing smile, his head wobbled, and he scraped a foldaway chair across the kitchen floor, which he landed on. 'Do you think that's because he doesn't want Mrs Ali to know what the shop's going to be?' Harold steepled his fingers as though there was a cunning plan afoot. Gemma's eyes darted from one fool to the other across the table.

'I think so, Harold, especially as Mrs Ali has promised me a discount on fags if I keep her updated as to what the shop is going to be.'

'He's given up smoking though… for me.' Gemma touched her midriff, patted Ricky Ricketts on the forearm, and looked at him with doe eyes. This was followed by searching around the room for Edith in the hope of sucking up to her new potential mother-in-law. Even though Edith would love to hear that her only son had given up smoking, she had escaped to the front room to watch her lunchtime quiz show (without Harold, who, as you know would ruin it for her).

'Ahh, so what are you going to do?' Harold stroked his chin. His dodgy skills had not been used since the wedding and were going to waste.

'Well,' said Gemma as Harold's glance batted her away.

'Well, I'll tell him, Gemma's a journalist for the

Manchester Evening News.'

'For the time being,' she interrupted.

'Yeah, so she can investigate what Mr Dubois plans to do with the shop, and I don't have to have anything to do with it; keep them both sweet.'

Harold liked the plan, nodding in pleased agreement (which is slightly different from his side to side head wobbling). But something had dawned on him. 'Hang on! Are you the same Gemma that Wantha was always falling out with Ricky over?'

'Yes, I probably am,' Gemma smirked a self-satisfied smirk.

'Are you the same Gemma that caused a fight at my wedding breakfast?' Harold thought back to the black eye in the Chinese restaurant.

'Oh, that wasn't her fault,' Ricky thumbed Gemma a shield.

'Well, that must mean that you're the same Gemma who did not run the story about my third place victory at the Black pudding throwing contest. Or my shock proposal to Edith at the charity pub quiz!'

Harold remembers everything, apart from his placing at the *World Black Pudding Throwing Championship*, which was more like fifth, than third. (And he had cheated by throwing the first one overarm).

'Oh, yes, sorry about that, but that last one, that's what made me hand my notice in at The Bury Times,' Gemma lied. 'The editor cut my story in two, that's why I left... I work for The Manchester Evening News now... for the time being.'

But it was too late; Harold wanted to include Edith in on the news of who this Jezebel really was.

'Edith! Edith! Can you come in here please?' Harold shouted. But Edith was just about to find out if Finoula from Dorset was going to scoop the jackpot on the lunch-time quiz show.

'Wait a minute,' Edith shouted back. Harold got up to investigate the hold-up, and as he rose from the chair, the tin of peaches he had bought from Marks and Spencer earlier was revealed on the counter behind him.

'Are they peaches?' Gemma excited. 'Oh, I've got such a craving for peaches!'

'I'm sure Harold won't mind,' said Ricky. Opening the tin, he passed them with a spoon to Gemma. (You can't expect her to eat them straight out of the tin, Ricky Ricketts). Edith and Harold returned to the kitchen to find Ricky Ricketts and an unreliable journalist eating Harold's peaches.

'My peaches!' shouted Harold, snatching them

out of Gemma Hampsons' hand.

'Sorry, I just had a craving,' Gemma moved her chair backwards and stroked her belly, which was as large and round as Wantha's had been in Marks and Spencer earlier.

'It's the baby, baby wanted peaches!' said Gemma straight into the wide and disbelieving eyes of Harold and Edith.

CHAPTER 11: FRENCH PEOPLE DO IT WITH THE LIGHTS ON.

On this particular evening at Chateau le Grincheaux, Edna and Genevieve's room was lit only by the setting French sun over the glorious expanse of beautiful landscape. Edna had really been getting used to this feeling of happiness and contentment. A feeling unfamiliar to her in the past few years. It was just short of a decade since Genevieve had fallen out with her adopted son, Matteo. This resulted in a supposed out of court settlement and Edna being unceremoniously dumped. But now Genevieve was back, and they had escaped to France, together again at last. Genevieve was reading one of Diane's historical fiction novels, coughing with each page turn. I do hope she was not spluttering on the pages, it was a Margaret Skea novel, so Diane would most likely want to reread it.

Meanwhile, Edna was lying there and thinking about how happy she was. What could possibly go wrong? Nothing Edna, stop being silly and worrying over nothing… cough, cough, page turn. Genevieve was already hidden under the high thread count Egyptian cotton linen. Edna was thinking mundane thoughts to pass the time until she fell to sleep…

What would she wear tomorrow? Maybe a dark coloured turtleneck and dark coloured slacks. No, that was the type of miserable outfit Edna didn't feel like wearing… did she? Turtlenecks are comfortingly protective, hiding her neck wrinkles. She must remember to pluck her grey whiskers from the bottom of her chin; they do show up against the dark of a turtleneck. No… No, not a turtleneck! Tomorrow, Edna would present herself as a flamboyant, exuberant, confident woman with no worries and nothing to hide (except a few lumps and bumps). She would wear her never-been-seen-before bright red, flowing caftan; slightly see-through, but not on purpose. Yes, that's what Edna would do tomorrow and would most probably team it with some carefree costume jewellery, oh how bohemian!

Edna glanced over at Genevieve, now asleep with Diane's book resting on her chest. Genevieve had refused to discuss Matteo since her reunion with Edna. 'What does it matter now?' Genevieve had said when Edna attempted to raise the subject in that little holiday cottage in Northumberland. The truth was, Edna was frightened. She feared that Genevieve was hiding something, although Edna had not wanted to know the truth. Remember that phone call between Edna and Genevieve when the cat, Henri the Third died? Edna was sure that another female had answered - a female with a Mancunian accent. Edna, having been alone for all that time, had not wanted to know who this new mystery female was. Don't forget, Edna had stalked Genevieve on Facebook… There had been a photograph of her with a French Poodle. Where was that dog now? And what of the debts that Genevieve had left Edna with? Also never mentioned; apart from Genevieve commenting that Edna must be 'doing very well for herself in this big house'.

But that was not so; Edna had been forced to live there in poverty, alone, without a sex life. With only her idiot sister, Edith and the imbecile Harold for company. Not to mention her disagreeable nephew, Ricky Ricketts and his rag-tag posse from the Hillock estate… (Err, cannot wait until Edna finds out about what's happened there).

Seemingly, Edna had landed at Chateau le Grincheaux with its English speaking hosts at Genevieve's pleasing. And they had not been out for days. They are meant to be escaping into the French experience, not hiding! And what about Genevieve? Not speaking French, not acting French either. Edna had not seen her perform one of those double kisses once since they had been here! She smokes, she coughs, and she hides behind her little smart two-piece suits. What has she got to hide? Genevieve turned over in her sleep, almost but not quite knocking the historical novel to the floor. The room was still awash with pink and orange light from the setting sun. Genevieve started coughing again, and Edna removed the resting book from her shoulders.

'Oh, pardon! Oh, I fell asleep there!' Genevieve sat up and sipped a bit of water. 'I'm sorry, did I wake you?'

'No,' Edna sighed, 'I was just thinking about what sort of outfit to wear tomorrow.'

'Ahh, another outfit suitable for another day of relaxation…' Genevieve kissed her fingers together in Edna's direction and then climbed fully under the cover. Edna joined her, and soon Genevieve's French fingers caressed Edna's Mancunian love handles. She pulled the blanket over both their heads and kissed Edna fully on the mouth with her smoky breath. They both sighed and held each other in an embrace for quite some time. Just as Edna got into a comfortable position, Genevieve whispered in her ear. 'Shut the blinds, mon amie.' The room was now in darkness. And as Genevieve's warm little hand slipped under Edna's pyjama top, she couldn't help thinking to herself... What is Genevieve hiding? French people do it with the lights on!

CHAPTER 12: MEANWHILE, ON CURMUDGEON AVENUE.

On this particular day in Whitefield, the air was full of secrets, revelations and suspicion. And this is not only because Ricky Ricketts' introduced the heavily pregnant Gemma.

'So, question is Ricky, are you going to make an honest woman of her?' Harry the Bastard was lugging rubbish sacks into the skip that Matteo had hired for the renovation of Number Three Curmudgeon Avenue. That's right, Ricky Ricketts had enlisted the help of his '*guy*' Harry the Bastard, formerly Harry the Jack-of-all-trades electrician. He had agreed to come out of retirement for this exceptional and secret project. Ricky emptied a few bricks out of his sack before heaving it into the skip. Matteo was never going to get anywhere with this weakling.

'Too heavy,' Ricky huffed.

'Never mind too heavy, put your back into it,' Harry said. Having at least two decades on Ricky, he was in much better shape. 'Are you going to do the right thing by her?'

'Oh, Gemma, no, there's no need.'

'No need? Take some advice from your old mate Harry; I have never met a woman who doesn't want to get married.'

'How many times have you been married again? Three, four?'

'Six if you include Imelda - she just moved in for a bit. I'm all heart, Ricky, and so are you, so I've heard!'

'What? Yeah, I am, but Gemma's the one who doesn't want to get married. She said she would rather name this baby with her surname than mine.'

'Can't say I blame her. Ha! Imagine if you'd married Wantha. Wantha Ricketts. Sounds like fertiliser or something, which is appropriate in her condition!'

'What condition?' said Ricky.

'Shhh! Less chatting, the boss is coming!' Harry raised his dirty forefinger to his lips because Matteo was on his way downstairs.

'Already looking great down here,' Matteo said. 'I've just got a few calls to make in the office, and then I'll pop out to the cafe for breakfast for the three of us. It's on me, of course.'

What a smoothy! Matteo knows how to keep people happy, just like his mother. He disappeared into his office and shut the door. Harry and Ricky continued to shovel a load of scrap into bags for the skip; Number Three Curmudgeon Avenue was to be completely cleaned out.

'Hey, what's this?' Ricky picked up a smallish piece of metal with little indentations in it, he held it up to his face like a mask, and then Harry the Bastard took it off him.

'This is one of those old cigarette grilles, like an ashtray for putting your cigarette out before you entered the house,' Harry frowned. 'I'm not sure where you would put your dimp, though.'

'Maybe people saved it for later? If it was in the old days, then maybe they just put it in their pocket. Eww, I can't believe I just put it up to my face!'

'No,' Harry stroked his hairy chin in thought, as though he was on an episode of *Time Team.* 'I bet it was for people to strike a match on, to light their pipe before they went *into* the house, that's it. Might be worth something.'

'I hear the *Antiques Roadshow* is going to the

Drill Hall up Bury, you should take it there.'

'Really?' Harry the Bastard smoothed down his beard.

'No, I'm just winding you up. You don't half make some crap up, Harry!'

'Cheeky, you start pulling that door frame off with that crow-bar.'

The two men continued with what people would pay good money for in some parts, as a stress-relieving day of demolition. It wasn't long before Ricky announced that yet again, he was knackered, and Matteo had been a rather long time in the office making his important calls.

'Do you think we should knock on and tell him we're ready for him to go to the caff?'

'No, don't do that; it's a liberty,' Harry winced. 'Although, he has been in there for a rather long time.'

The two of them edged forward to see if they could hear anything. There was nothing at first, just the silent sound of life on Curmudgeon Avenue.

'What did you mean before about Wantha being in a condition?' Ricky whispered. Harry shushed him as Matteo's important phone calls were now audible through the office door.

'How's my favourite girl? Look at you! Dirty

girl! What have you been up to?'

'OMG! He's got someone in there!' Ricky whispered.

'Shush Ricky,' Harry the Bastard went all wide-eyed on him.

'Can any girl ever look as cute as you? You're sooooooo beautiful! I've got something for you!' Matteo could be heard saying. Both men realised their uncomfortable eavesdropping, although Ricky thought that if his mother listens in on conversations, then it must be alright. They slowly turned and started tiptoeing away from the office door when it happened.

'Oh, you're a dirty girl. Grrrrrr!' Matteo was making a gruff sound, which went on for longer than was reasonably necessary. Ricky Ricketts and Harry the Bastard made a dash for it out of Number Three Curmudgeon Avenue's front door.

'The dirty bastard!' said Harry the Bastard.

'Toonan said there was summat funny about him. I feel bad now for taking the piss out of her!'

Edith, who of course, had been trying to listen (unsuccessfully) to the goings-on next door, opened her own front door and invited Ricky and Harry in for a cup of tea. Having finished his important phone calls, Matteo opened his office door to find himself alone. Oh, he thought, breakfast for one then? He only had himself to blame for hiring Ricky Ricketts, but that way, he got to have a bit of fun with Mrs Ali, plus keep his new neighbours, Harold and Edith sweet.

Although seemingly, those two were never happy.

CHAPTER 13: DIANE AND JACKSON'S ROAD TRIP

'Ah, bonjour!' Genevieve greeted Diane and Jackson; they were loading their car up for what seemed to be a big trip. Thermos flasks with blue and pink cups... A picnic basket... Picnic blankets... Water and sunhats and all kinds of paraphernalia. Diane pursed her lips when she took in the scene of Genevieve taking over her terrace with her skinny body, cocktail glass and cigarettes. Diane was convinced that Genevieve had been topless sunbathing in the middle of the day, she just knew it.

Although renting out space in their chateau brought Mr and Mrs Bove a tidy sum, Diane was getting rather bored of sharing their home. Mr

Bove was oblivious, as husbands sometimes are.

'Anyone would think we're going away for the weekend!' Jackson laughed, and so did Genevieve in agreement. Diane could not help noticing her husband's eyes glancing at the fallen shoulder straps of Genevieve's two-piece.

'Where are yooo going?' Genevieve Frenched it up for Mr Bove's benefit.

'Oh, we're going to Rocamadour,' Jackson said. Genevieve choked on her cigarette.

Naked Edna popped her head out of her bedroom window, her hands across her bare wrinkly breasts.

'Rocamadour!!!' she shrieked. 'Wait! Wait for me! For us! Oh, Genevieve, let's go with them today!' Edna could be heard running back into her bedroom, caftans and costume jewellery flying everywhere, accompanied by more coughing and spluttering from a half-dressed Genevieve. Diane's eyes were ablaze at Jackson. If only he had turned down the volume on his voice.

'Oh, we thought we would give you a bit of privacy, let you enjoy the chateau all to yourselves, you don't want us two hanging around all day - we're not even French!' Diane laughed and gave an unconscious sideways glance towards Genevieve's perfect, albeit wrinkly physique.

'Ah merci, merci,' Genevieve brightened as

Edna burst through the French doors looking nuts with a face of expectation.

'Oh, you're still here! Oh, thank goodness!' Edna said, taking a liberty, she opened the back passenger door of the Bove's car and sat down, flicking through a French atlas. 'Genevieve, put some clothes on for goodness sakes. Mr and Mrs Bove will want to set off; I can't tell from this map how long it will take us to get there.'

'Us?' Diane whispered to Jackson.

'Edna,' Jackson said, gently demonstrating that he was able to talk quietly. He leant over the side of the car, bobbing his head slightly inside. 'The thing is, I, we hope you don't mind, but the thing is I was hoping to take my wife to Rocamadour for a romantic day out. You know, just the two of us.'

Edna ignored Jackson and silently perused a French tour guide.

'Do you know, this book hardly mentions Rocamadour,' Edna lifted her head, and despite being at a lower position than Jackson, managed to turn her nose up at him. 'I'm sorry, did you say something?'

'GET OOT OF THE CAR!' Diane swung the car door open at the other side. Genevieve's mouth formed an amused 'O' shape.

'I'm sorry?' Edna said indignantly raising her

shoulders.

'Let me handle this,' Jackson gently pulled his wife away.

'Psst, psst,' Genevieve beckoned Diane over to her sun lounger. 'I, erm, I really don't wish to go on a day trip today. I have been feeling unwell. I would rather stay 'ere.'

'Well, yes, look, I'm sorry I just, I just well, I wanted a day out with Jackson.'

'Of course, mon amie, of course.'

'Well, how are we going to... Oh! Here she comes now!'

Edna came skipping over towards Genevieve and Diane as Jackson stood next to the car, grinning. She put both her arms around Diane and kissed her on both cheeks. Genevieve nodded at Diane to say, '*make a dash for it while you can.*' Diane made her way to the car.

'I don't know what you said to Edna, but well done, husband,' Diane enthused.

'Well, I told a wee fib. I told her that it's our anniversary.'

'Oh, well, then! I'll be wanting an anniversary present!'

'Aye, I'll probably have to buy you one. Especially as I've promised we would take them back to Rocamadour next week after we have sampled the most romantic places...'

CHAPTER 14: IF THERE'S A MILLIONAIRE IN RADCLIFFE, THEN PATCHOULI WILL FIND HIM.

Mr and Mrs Bove were driving as fast as they could away from the Chateau le Grincheaux. Ricky Ricketts and Harry the Bastard were knee-deep in builder's rubble, and Harold and Edith were hiding in their bedroom. Away from the downstairs drama (they were convinced that Ricky could bring yet another pregnant woman to sit at their Formica kitchen table at any moment).

While all this was going on, Toonan and her

mother Patchouli decided that something was missing in their lives… Romance. A fan of all things instantaneous, Toonan had researched local speed dating events. She found one, reasonably local to them, in, of all places, the back room of the Bridge Tavern in Radcliffe. New owners had taken over since Harold had moved to Curmudgeon Avenue, and they were trying all kinds to get the punters in. Patchouli had been researching men for decades but was going along to support her daughter. Wantha had decided to stay at home on account of her condition.

Now, I don't need to tell you how speed dating works, although, being a Victorian house in Whitefield, you cannot expect me to know all the ins and outs. Before bells started ringing, flirtations and boxes began being ticked; Toonan and Patchouli got themselves a couple of drinks. Toonan was on the cider, and Patchouli sipped a gin.

'Hello everyone, and thank you for joining us in the Bridge Tavern's very first speed dating night!' said the landlady. Patchouli and Toonan stared at each other in excited anticipation.

'Could I ask the male participating speed daters to sit at these individual tables? Ladies, (she glanced over at Toonan at this point), please collect a dating card and pen on your way to your first date.'

'Did she used to be a school teacher?' Patchouli whispered.

'Great, now, let the speed dating begin! Oh, I forgot to say, move on to your next date after I ring the bell.'

'These dates will be some of the longest relationships I've ever had!' Toonan said to her mother, but Patchouli had already disappeared to the first table. Considering she was just there to support Toonan, Patchouli was the first to get stuck in.

'Hello, I'm Patchouli, pleased to meet you,' she began, having picked someone a similar age to herself.

'Pleased to meet you too; I'm Benjamin. What a beautiful name, I'm very impressed with how you express yourself...'

'Come again?' asked Patchouli, losing her seductive vocalisations. Benjamin nodded at her clothes.

'I see you like the dark arts... I used to be a Goth myself, back in the day,' Benjamin fumbled under his shirt for a chain suspending an upside-down cross. Patchouli was devastated.

'How dare you! I'm a metal-head, a rock chick! I can assure you BENJAMIN that I never have, and never will crimp my hair,' Patchouli adjusted her biker jacket and turned to the hostess. 'Ring your bell, love, times up!'

They all moved around one, Toonan avoiding her mother's reject, landed in front of her new date.

'Alrite, I'm Toonan, pleased to meet you,' she reached out and shook the hand of a rather timid-looking male.

'Hello. I'm Paul. What did you say your name was again?'

'Toonan. My mum made it up.'

'Oh, that's... unusual... erm my mum used to call me Small Paul,' he said, clutching at the straws of common ground.

'That's nice,' Toonan didn't know what to say, but Small Paul, despite his apparent fears, had done this before.

'So, have you done this before?' Small Paul leaned forward to ask her just that.

'What speed dating? Haha, is that your way of asking me if I come here often?' Toonan had been told not to be too sweet but include a bit of banter (you guessed right, she had been to the Wantha school of dating earlier tonight).

'Well, have you?' asked Small Paul.

'No!' Toonan said, stunned.

'I have. I've done every speed dating event from my home town of Todmorden and back again.' Small Paul looked wistfully into the corner of the room, almost with a tear in his eye. Toonan opened her mouth to speak, but the bell rang, and it was move-around again time. Patchouli sat down in front of a cowboy hat (who wears a cowboy hat at a speed dating event?).

'Hello, I'm Patchouli,' she held out her hand, which was instantly grabbed and uncomfortably kissed by the grey bristles of a moustache grazing her fingers.

'I'm Maurice,' he said (OMG! Remember him!) His voice rumbled like a motorbike. Patchouli snatched her hand away, leaned backwards, and through squinted eyes she asked;

'Don't I know you? You look familiar.'

Two tables away, Maurice had been recognised by Toonan. Ignoring her current date (Jonathan, the joiner from Crumpsall), she desperately tried to get her mother's attention.

'No! Mum! No! That's the bloke that murdered Ediff and Edna's cat!' (Don't forget, Toonan knew all about it because she had bumped into the two sisters at Whitefield police station). Fortunately, the bell rang; Maurice had convinced Patchouli that her recognition of him had been a *'false memory'*. She agreed but proceeded to tell him about being a vulnerable adult (too right, Patchouli, now get yourself away from that murderer!).

Time to move again and Toonan was exhausted. 'Wotcha,' she flopped herself down on the chair.

'Alrite Toonan, I've not seen you for time!' Neil said. It turned out he had known Toonan since primary school.

'Neil? I thought you were married?' Toonan said.

'Oh, that, yeah, me and Debs, we're just trying something different at the moment, to spice things up. So if you fancy it?' Neil wiggled his eyebrows at Toonan.

'What? No!' But Toonan's eyes were once again distracted by her dating expert mother, Patchouli. She was laughing, laughing at anything her date said, and touching! Gently touching his forearm every time he spoke.

'Oh, I see your mum's copped with Gil Von Black.'

'Who?' Toonan and Neil gazed over at the pair; a man dressed head to toe in leather, with long grey hair and tinted aviator sunglasses, Patchouli in her new floor-length dress and skull-adorned scarf.

'He's loaded, used to be a session guitarist back in the day. All the greats, Black Sabbath, Metallica erm... I even think he played with Def Leppard once!'

'Fuck me,' said Toonan.

'I know, he's a property developer now,' said Neil. Then the bell rang.

'Hang on, I haven't had the chance to say,' Neil reached out and grabbed Toonan by the shell suit. 'Saw your Wantha the other day. Is she pregnant?'

'Oh, it's a long story...' Toonan rolled her eyes. 'Sees ya later, say hi to Debs for me.'

Toonan thought it was time to move on to another table and met with the eyes of another Radcliffe love punter who scurried away from the scene. 'What?' she said, but the speed dating was over.

'Thanks, guys, I think it's been a success.' The speed dating hostess gushed towards Patchouli and Gil.

'Hang on; I haven't had the chance to...' Toonan looked down at her own blank card.

'Not to worry, honey,' she beckoned Toonan over. Small Paul had ticked that he liked Toonan on his card!

Patchouli and Toonan made their way home in a taxi and met a very sulky looking Wantha.

'Alright, howdya get on then?'

'Mum's pulled this old rocker. What's he called again?'

'Gil,' Patchouli blushed.

'Yeah, he's worth a few quid too apparently,' Toonan said, much to her mother's disgust. 'You should go shoplifting in Marks and Spencer more often, Sis!'

'I know, I told you, look rich, attract money,' Wantha said, in her leopard print onesie.

'I do wish you would stop pretending to be pregnant though, I don't even know why you would want Ricky Ricketts back,' said Toonan.

'I know,' said Patchouli. 'Look pregnant attract…'

'A shitty nappy,' Toonan finished.

'Shut up, Toonan! Right, anyway, I won't have to. I forgot to tell you, guess who I saw in Marks and Spencer the other day.'

'Who?'

'Harold and Ediff!' Wantha said triumphantly. 'I had to avoid them because of my phantom pregnancy.'

'Aww, I miss those two,' said Toonan without batting an eyelid.

'So do I. Go on then love, you get Ricky Ricketts back, then we can see Harold and Edith again,' agreed Patchouli.

'Hang on, I got chosen too!' Toonan said. 'Yeah, Small Paul from Todmorden ticked my box!'

'He might have love, but I saw him speeding away from the pub in his Hyundai Hatchback.'

CHAPTER 15: JE REGRETTE.

Yet again, during this particular sunset in France, the deep orange and pink sky blanketed the surrounding landscape and occasional buildings. And yet again, Edna Payne and Madame Genevieve Dubois were in bed. However, this time, Edna was asleep (bread, cheese, wine and crushed up antihistamines will do that to you). The deep colours of the sky reflected Genevieve's regretful eyes. She had not thought her life through, but then who does?

Most people go with the flow, like Edna's sister Edith. Taking whatever life throws at them until they end up living in the house they grew up in with their new husband, (who cannot stop moaning). Some folk (like Gemma) discover an unwanted pregnancy and clutch on to the only sure bet they have in the local area. People don't plan. So you cannot blame Genevieve for taking things as they come. It is not your fault, Genevieve; think of yourself, think of the here and now. You are back in France; you are living in a beautiful chateau. Edna has forgiven you, has she not? Genevieve did not know; Edna had only spoken of superficial things.

Never mind, you can have a superficial relationship, now go to sleep, Genevieve, you have a big day ahead of you tomorrow. You must get up early and convince Edna that you should take on a new hobby. She had said they are escaping, not hiding, had she not? Yes, she had, fine, Genevieve, you give in to Edna's demands. You agree to go out; your new joint hobby is hiking. You and Edna can walk for miles and miles in the beautiful French countryside.

You will hike up hillsides; you will saunter down country lanes you will perhaps go skinny dipping in a stream, like a scene from one of Cezanne's *Bathers*. And maybe, you will throw in a sprained ankle. Then you will not have to return to Rocamadour. Or better still, Edna gets the sprained ankle… All those steps cannot be managed with a sprained ankle. Parfait! Now you can sleep, Genevieve.

But Genevieve could not sleep. She lay there, listening to Edna's noises, her wind, her snoring, and her breathing. Perhaps it was her failure to address the past that was keeping Genevieve awake? Genevieve did not like confrontation. When Matteo threatened to reveal all her secrets, she had created an entirely new set of secrets. Genevieve convinced Edna that Matteo had settled out of court regarding his lack of adoption papers. There was no such court case, but Genevieve had given Matteo a modest sum of money to shut him up, she had his promise, and she had left Matteo knowing half the story.

Matteo may have threatened to out his adopted mother, but how could he? Not knowing the truth himself. Only Genevieve knew what happened. She had ended up running all the way back to France with the rest of the money (which did not last long.) She changed her name, changed everything about herself, now a dog lover, rather than a cat lover. Even so, she was left with hardly anything, despite what the newspapers said about her. Those three men died of natural causes, she had just been unlucky, and life insurance? A pittance and it doesn't count if you are not officially married. Deciding against revealing any of her many truths to Edna, Genevieve tried again to go back to sleep. But she could not. Why had she acted the way that she had all her life? A young girl's shame had not needed to last as long as it had, surely. And now, why should she still feel the same?

What was shameful then is not shameful now, the act of love, romance and ultimate lust. For a woman who had loved many, Madame Genevieve Dubois should have nothing to be ashamed of. Well, she would not have, had she not dragged everyone down with her. Matteo did not deserve to be moved around England, never settling and not knowing who he was. Not knowing the truth about his own mother. What she had done in that French convent was rescue the sleeping snuffling baby. Genevieve thought she was saving him. Stealing him away before the nuns stole him away from her. Then, Genevieve carried on pretending that she had adopted him - why?

She enjoyed it, that's why. How noble, how dignified it had seemed, a single French woman with that attractive accent saving the life of a needy Parisian orphan...

When Matteo was born, so too was Madame Genevieve Dubois. Maybe Matteo on her mind was keeping her awake. Genevieve had given him everything, everything she could apart from the truth.

Genevieve hoped that Francesca had finally agreed to marry Matteo. Maybe he had a little family of his own now; she regretted this would be a family she would never get to see. Genevieve could not risk going back to Britain, back to England, the north, Whitefield, and Curmudgeon Avenue. She glanced over at Edna, now silently turned on her side, oh she did love her and regretted leaving her for all that time, but she had no choice. In six days, Genevieve must choose *not* to go on a trip to Rocamadour without Edna becoming suspicious. Genevieve's choices were slimming down as fast as her figure.

CHAPTER 16: WHITEFIELD'S VERY OWN ASIAN MISS MARPLE (WITH STYLE)

The last time we saw Matteo, his office was full of noises that made Ricky Ricketts and Harry the Bastard very suspicious. Sounds that had not been heard on Curmudgeon Avenue for quite some time, some may say for longer than was reasonably necessary. Men being men, the noises had not been mentioned since. Despite this, the renovation of Number Three Curmudgeon Avenue had proceeded in relative silence. But outside of work, Ricky had been bursting at the seams. His mother and Mrs Ali had both hounded him for information regarding the goings-on under Mr Dubois' roof. But neither Ricky nor Harry could say anything. They were both sworn to secrecy and did not want to risk losing their cash-in-hand building job.

'Morning lads, wow! You're doing a great job here, can't believe how quickly you're getting through the renovations!' Matteo lied, passing cups of tea to both the men. 'Three sugars, wasn't it, Ricky?'

'Err yeah,' Ricky nodded.

'Last night, I took delivery of a very special package. When I show it to you two, you will understand why I needed it to be delivered under cover of night… and it might remind you of why I asked you both to keep things hush-hush.'

The work-shy pair had already downed tools to drink their brews. What was Matteo was about to reveal?

'Step into my office, gents, and we shall begin.' (Matteo is so damn smooth!)

While all this was going on, the lesser spotted Wantha was making her return on foot to Curmudgeon Avenue. Her glorious afro like a mane, her skin, her clothes, her… everything. Wantha Rose arrived like a repatriated Benin Bronze, cradling her extended stomach as though there was a precious cargo aboard. There was something different about her, today of all days when Ricky Ricketts was right here, inside one of these very houses. Too scared to enter the back office for fear of his new boss's perversions...

Wantha thought better of going around the back, especially after ignoring Edith and Harold up Bury the other day. She raised her eyebrows, batted her false lashes, plumped her voluptuous lips, and raised one hand to knock the brass door knocker. (Wow, look at those gem-encrusted gel nails! Fancy). Fancy but futile, Wantha. Harold and Edith are not in.

Meanwhile, Matteo was waiting for his two employees in his office. Harry the Bastard, having shifted his allegiance from *Game of Thrones* to *American Horror Story,* knew all too well how these things worked. He barred Ricky from entering the office with the palm of his hand against Ricky's chest.

'Hang on,' he nodded. Then, with his work gloves rolled into a sausage and held in both hands, Harry knocked on Matteo's door.

'Ah! Well, come in then, I've got the first of many boxes here!' Matteo said from behind his sleek black office desk.

'Well, we just thought it might be better if you came out here to show us...' If Harry the Bastard were wearing a cap, he would have doffed it.

'Yeah, we don't want any funny business,' Ricky said, placing his foot in his mouth.

'Funny business! What's that supposed to mean?' Matteo laughed a dismissive laugh. Getting up from his executive leather chair, he grabbed the heavy box off the floor. Harry hit Ricky Ricketts with his rolled-up work gloves and made emergency eyes.

'Better light out here, boss...' Harry said, but Matteo was ready to make an announcement...

'I knew, I knew when I met you two, especially you, Ricky, that I had met my future mates. I need you, and you need me.' Towering above both men with handsome presidency, Matteo Dubois reached inside the cardboard box for the loot he was desperate to show them.

Meanwhile, Wantha Rose, who did not like wasting her time, was gutted that there had been no answer from Harold and Edith. Patchouli had told her to get Ricky back in her life, and that's what she had decided to do. Edith, Wantha had decided, would be the lynchpin in her plot, the person most likely to fall for her charms. But Edith was not at home, and Wantha had made such an effort. She had spent all her money on her appearance when she should have been buying herself a new phone. (I thought there was something different about her! No phone!) Then again, she should not have lost her temper and thrown her old phone against the wall and smashed it into a thousand pieces, all because of Gemma Hampsons' status updates on Instagram '#baby #Ricky-Ricketts'BabyMama #threemonthstogo'.

Wantha had borrowed Toonan's phone and Instagram account to add her response. A photo of herself, seemingly pregnant, but with no caption. Not even a hashtag, so she had not lied, not really. Yet one Instagram post is enough to start a thousand rumours; you know what Whitefield gossip is like!

Speaking of which, here comes Mrs Ali, outside the most popular shop in Whitefield, outside, and under the pretence of cleaning her windows.

'Darling!' she said, arms outstretched to Wantha. 'Darling, I have missed you! Oh, you look beautiful, darling. Absolutely stunning.'

'Alrite Mrs Ali,' Wantha said. Mrs Ali's compliments seemed like a waste of her efforts, and she walked back down Harold and Edith's front path. 'You seen Harold and Ediff today?'

'Yes darling, they've gone to Bleakholt Animal Sanctuary to look at the cats and dogs.'

'Aww, they getting a pet?'

'What do you think? I'm not taking any bets as to whether Harold lets Edith get a cat, the last one they had at that house was her sister's.'

'Oh right, the one that got murdered...'

'You've come to see Ricky, haven't you, really?'

Mrs Ali gestured towards Wantha's belly. 'I hear congratulations are in order...' Mrs Ali narrowed her eyes and gripped Wantha's elbow. 'Or are they?'

'What?' Wantha turned her body away from the all-knowing Mrs Ali, who herself had a thought to turn this exchange to her benefit.

'Never mind, darling... have you been around the back?'

'No,' Wantha's demeanour lost the fake pregnancy bump at the front of her body. Mrs Ali raised an '*I knew it*' eyebrow. She linked arms with Wantha.

'I think we should go and have a look around the back then, put your mind at rest, no point having a wasted journey after you have gone to such a beautiful effort on your appearance.'

Wantha pretended she had something in her eye as the two women made their way down my side. She did have something, a tear, the worst kind of tear, the tear of heartbreak (wasted if you ask me on the likes of Ricky Ricketts).

When Matteo first surprised Ricky Ricketts and Harry the Bastard with the precious cargo from his mysterious box, both pairs of dirty Whitefield eyes were deceived. It must have been the way Matteo was holding it; his sexy fingers cradled the impressive phallic-shaped object, dangling it in front of him for both men to see.

'Now, this, gents is top quality meat,' Matteo said. 'The best way of testing salami is to hold it in your right hand, suspend it loosely, and have a good feel of the girth and weight.' Mr Matteo Dubois had a way of making everything sound tempting. Yet, he was also full of the unfounded. He knew nothing about salami because Matteo had never, ever worked in a delicatessen in all his life... but he wanted to... Enter Number Three Curmudgeon Avenue!

'Come on then, you two have a go,' Matteo grinned at both men. The three of them stood inside the backroom window, fondling their salamis. At precisely the same moment, Wantha and Mrs Ali broke into Harold and Edith's back yard. They were now standing on a bench and peeping over the wall. (In the same way that Matteo had to Harold and Edith). Both women gasped... unseen by the males; they could hardly believe their eyes at the three bobbing members next door.

'No... it can't be,' whispered Wantha. 'I mean, I can't speak for the tall, handsome, smartly dressed man, but that is definitely not the original article on Ricky Ricketts,' Wantha whispered.

'Oh, well, that explains everything,' said Mrs Ali (she had, of course, explained to Wantha that the fraud investigator was really called Matteo and was opening a shop).

'What? What does it explain?' said Wantha, still staring at the window.

'They... Are dildos! Mr Matteo Dubois, previously the tall, handsome stranger... is opening a sex shop, and Ricky Ricketts and Harry the Bastard will work there!' Mrs Ali concluded in defiance. 'I've worked it all out.'

'I love you, Mrs Ali. You're like an Asian Miss Marple,' Wantha laughed.

'With style darling, with style,' Mrs Ali nodded and adjusted her stylish sash.

CHAPTER 17: THE POODLE THAT UPSET THE HORNET'S NEST.

On this particular day in France, it was lovely weather for a walk in the countryside. Remember when I told you that Edna had only spoken to Genevieve superficially about the events of their separated decade? That was because Edna deemed Genevieve a flight risk. She had left once before, and there was nothing to stop her from flying again. (Edna was not to know that Genevieve was trapped in France, unable to risk the channel crossing again for fear of arrest).

Edna's fear of displeasing Genevieve was so strong that she had agreed to go on this countryside hike with her. You read that correctly; Edna Payne had decided to go on a walk with Genevieve Dubois, a long one.

'Ah see, my love,' Genevieve playfully wrapped her arms around the majority of Edna's middle. What a good idea walking had been. It was a beautiful day in a beautiful country. Mr and Mrs Bove had been thrilled to bits when the pair of lovers had announced their intentions for the day and politely declined to join them.

'Do you remember when we first met?' Genevieve asked. Both women had been guilty of adopting this line of questioning when romance was required. 'You were walking that day. You had walked all the way from... Prestwich.'

'Oh, haha, oh not quite, just the other side of Whitefield if I remember rightly. I was going to Maurice's art group. Oh, Genevieve, you do know he was the one responsible for Henri the Third's death?' Edna could not remember if this had come up in conversation when she had tried to contact Genevieve at the time, and that reminded Edna of something.

'Oh! Non! My poor pussy cat.'

'I'm sorry you trusted me to look after him.'

'It's okay; you weren't to know Maurice was a cat murderer. How strange, though.'

(Ah, if only they knew the truth).

'I do remember it was raining that day when you walked into my life,' said Edna.

'Ah yes, and there had been a bit of life

drawing,' Genevieve purred, and the two women laughed. 'I had never done anything as brazen as that before, my Edna.'

'Really, well, to tell you the truth, I modelled myself on you from that day,' Edna said. 'Yes, I was like a bottle of bubble bath before I met you, and you were like a sophisticated French perfume. I remember thinking that there was nothing more elegant than a French lover at the time.'

The two women held hands and walked further along the country road, garnished either side by sunflower fields or the occasional tree. There was no way that Genevieve could tell Edna the truth now, not all of the truth, anyway.

As the two of them turned a wind in the road, a family with a dog approached them. They were walking rather swiftly. It must have been some sort of family power walking day out.

'Bonjour,' Edna sang, Genevieve just smiled.

'Alore! Don't go any further. Our dog has disturbed a hornet's nest; there are thousands of them, we have had to run!' The father of the family spoke in alarmed French. Genevieve mumbled something in return, in broken French that meant absolutely nothing to the family. Edna smiled, oblivious to the whole situation. The two carried on walking, despite the family repeating their warnings. They had no choice to remove themselves, their children and their French poodle from the scene.

'What were they saying, Genevieve?'

'Ah, they were saying they were in a rush because, erm, their dog needed the toilet, and they had forgotten to bring a poo bag.' Genevieve had to make something up. She had no clue what the man had said to her, such had been her absence from French-speaking company. 'And I said what a lovely dog.'

'Oh haha, oh, well, surely it would have been alright for the dog to go in the long grass, plenty of it around here,' Edna said, and Genevieve shrugged. But Edna had been reminded of something. She had spied on Genevieve's Facebook account when they were apart. It had appeared that Genevieve had a French poodle of her own… How could Edna get that into their conversation without revealing her spying behaviour?

'Dogs are lovely, aren't they?' this was all Edna could manage. 'Do you think you'd like a pet dog?'

'Ah, I've always preferred cats, my love. Who knows, mon amie, in the fullness of time, there might be room for a Henri the Fourth!' Genevieve said. 'Oh, ooo is this now? What is it you say in England? It is like Piccadilly Circus around here!'

A farmer, who appeared to be driving his tractor in a desperate fashion, approached the two women from the other side of the hedging.

'Don't go any further, madames,' he spoke in French. 'A family has just alerted me there is a disturbed hornet's nest ahead! I wouldn't want you to get stung!'

'Hahahaha, oh! Non-monsieur!' Genevieve laughed, and Edna laughed too, even though she had no clue what had just transgressed.

'What did he say?' said Edna.

'Oh, he asked if we had seen a dog pooping in his field. I said no because we hadn't had we?' Genevieve breathed a sigh of relief as she had managed to keep up her facade. The two of them continued their walk. They had not been out that long, after all. It had only been a matter of five or ten minutes before the sauntering pair met with the fate the French natives were trying to protect them from, and it was nothing to do with dog dirt.

'What are they?' Edna screamed. 'Oh, oh Genevieve, save me, those two are having sex!' Edna pointed at what appeared to be a mating pair of hornets. They were more likely flying in paired drones, their attack pheromone triggered by the French poodle.

'Oh, they're as big as mice!' Genevieve cried, swatting the beasties away from herself and from Edna. The two women clutched on to one another in the middle of France, surrounded by their own personal horror movie.

Later that same hour, the two women had power walked to the Chateau le Grincheaux as fast as their mismatched legs could carry them. Genevieve was blind in her left eye due to the swelling of an eyelid sting, and Edna had multiple bites on her limbs due to her loose-fitting tunic.

'Oh, my goodness!' Diane encouraged the two women to sit on her terrace furniture.

'Oh, hornets, hornets! They attacked us!' Edna wailed. 'French wasps! They are evil!' Edna was affronted. Genevieve clutched her (temporarily) blind face.

'Aye, the old farmer has been going round in his tractor warning folk,' said Jackson. 'Apparently, a dog upset a nest or some such tale, that'll be what caused it. They only sting when they've been attacked.'

'Oh, non-monsieur, French hornets will sting anybody,' Genevieve diverted the conversation. But Edna looked at her with an all-knowing look.

Ah well, another day is done, at least (temporarily) blind Genevieve has a good excuse not to go to Rocamadour.

CHAPTER 18: TOONAN'S NEW JOB.

Big changes had happened with Patchouli and her girls in their house on the Hillock estate. Wantha, as you know, spent a couple of months pining for that disagreeable twerp Ricky Ricketts. She had comfort eaten her way through her entire carer's allowance. Her stomach grew bigger and bigger. Wantha had now decided against a life of self-pity and was determined to get Ricky Ricketts back. Gemma Hampsons and her legitimate pregnancy was the only thing standing in Wantha's way. Every time Wantha thought about Ricky cheating on her, she could not bear it. But more about that later…

After accompanying her daughter to the Bridge Tavern's very first speed-dating night, Patchouli made a successful yet unexpected connection with Gil Von Black, the actual rock star.

He had been hiding in plain sight in Whitefield. Gil was now a property developer, and dripping in money (although Patchouli, the later life rocker, was not materialistic).

And what of Toonan Rose? Well, she is currently cleaning toilets for a Whitefield based cleaning company called The Mobile Mopheads which serves the entire Borough of Bury and beyond. Her sister was in some sort of weird love triangle. Her mother was in the grips of a whirlwind romance with a male specimen who had shared studio space with none other than Def Leppard. And Toonan Rose was just about to get her orders from Elsie, who had cleaned more toilets in her time, and so was slightly superior to Toonan. Elsie and Toonan made a good team, and Toonan enjoyed her new job. Elsie drove the van, and Toonan carried the cleaning kit in its bucket like plastic tub.

'You nip upstairs and start on the toilets, and I'll give all this woodwork a good polish,' said Elsie. The nifty duo had arrived in Bury town centre's one and only performing arts venue, The Met. With no parking directly outside, Toonan had the task of carrying all those cleaning supplies along Market Street. And now she had to drag them upstairs. The same staircase that Elsie had assigned herself the task of polishing.

Phew! Toonan was glad that was over, and

when she commenced her journey downstairs, she noticed there had been a lift all along! Flippin' heck! Toonan pressed the down button, and a woman in long skirts with beautiful long curly hair came running towards the lift area.

'Hold the lift, please!' she said. Toonan admired her ability to float along swiftly without tripping over a large cardboard cut out of a fairy.

'Oh, thank goodness!' the woman said, as the two of them got into the lift, 'I didn't even spot this lift the first day I worked here. I'd been going up and down the stairs with my cardboard fairies all day!'

'Same,' said Toonan. 'But without the fairies.' She so wanted to ask what the woman was doing, but the single floor journey in the lift would only allow for passing pleasantries... Usually, that is.

Despite recent renovations in the much-loved building, the two women heard a sound they were not expecting... It was the awful sound of the lift halting in rather a noisy and turbulent fashion. The two women laughed nervously; maybe the elevator always sounded like that. That was until they pressed the door-open button, and to their horror, discovered it would only open a tiny crack and appeared to be jammed between floors.

'Oh, no! I think we're stuck!' said Toonan.

'Oh, no!' the woman stood up, and her cardboard cut out fairy slid to the floor, and she started desperately pushing the buttons in the lift. 'What did you press?'

'What?' said Toonan.

'What did you press just now, before the doors opened that tiny bit?' she looked at Toonan in an accusatory fashion. Toonan was used to this; she totally looked like someone who would purposely push a button and make a lift break down, even if her self-care had improved since starting this cleaning job. Toonan just had a look about her, a look of mischief.

'I just pressed the 'doors open' button because I thought we'd stopped.' Toonan raised both hands in the air as though the lift lady was pointing a gun at her. Toonan's innocent demeanour made the other woman change hers.

'Oh, I'm sorry... sorry, it's obviously not your fault. I just feel a bit anxious about being trapped in here.'

'Trapped?! The door's open a little bit; I'm sure I can force it open,' Toonan was not about to admit lift defeat. 'Give me a leg up, will you?'

The other woman awkwardly put her hands around Toonan's middle and tried to lift her without putting in any real effort. Then Toonan showed her by linking her fingers together.

'I'll put my foot in your hands, and then you

stand up, then the force should catapult me into the air,' Toonan said. The other woman looked at her with a look of fear.

'Maybe we should try and phone someone first,' the other woman said. 'Can't you ring your boss? Will she be in the office?'

'Huh? No, we are mobile cleaners, whatchacall it – contracted. Anyway, I've no phone with me, I lent it to our Wantha, she smashed her phone when she found out her boyfriend had cheated on her, but now she's trying to get him back,' Toonan said.

'Who's Wantha? What a strange... sorry I've never met anyone called Wantha before,' the other woman said (you got *that* from that?!)

'Wantha's my sister, and I know... our mum made our names up. I'm Toonan, by the way. I won't shake your hand cos I've just been cleaning the toilets.'

'Oh,' the other woman withdrew her greeting. 'I'm Francesca,' she smiled. 'My mum told me she wanted to call me and my sister Tuscany and Savannah, so, you know!'

'What's your mum called?'

'Barbara.'

'Ah, my mum's called Patricia really, but she changed it to Patchouli.'

'Oh,' Francesca raised her eyebrows. 'Like

those incense sticks?'

'Summat like that. Right, shall we give this a go? The other cleaner, Elsie is out there… I'll shout her,' Toonan looked at Francesca, who was looking at Toonan's feet (she had just been cleaning the toilets, remember). 'OK, I'll take my trainers off,' Toonan said.

I don't know what was worse for Francesca, holding Toonan's trainers or her damp socks.

'Elsie! Elsie!' Toonan shouted… No answer.

'Sorry, I can't hold you for long!' Francesca said as both women almost stumbled onto the floor.

'Where's your phone then?' Toonan said, a bit breathless from the slight exertion.

'Oh, I left it upstairs… I try not to look at it too much.' Francesca was surprised at how easy it was to open up to Toonan.

'You split up with your boyfriend too?' Toonan put her head on one side.

'Is it that obvious?' Francesca lowered her head.

'It's a gift, Mum's psychic too, only I try not to use my powers,' Toonan said, matter of factly. 'Bit nosy innit.'

Francesca laughed and wiped a premature tear away.

'Blimey, I wish I had a biscuit tin and a cup of

tea!' said Toonan. 'That's what Mum does if she has to give anyone advice. Come on, let's try again.'

The procedure of hoisting Toonan up to the small crack the door and floor had created was easier the second time. And fortunately, Elsie heard them and knew just who to phone (she promised).

'Won't be long now!' Elsie shouted into the lift and then returned minutes later, having acquired some cans of pop, which she threw through the hole. 'Don't open them straight away; the fizz will go everywhere, and then we'll have to clean it, Toonan.'

The two women made themselves as comfortable as possible and anticipated their potential rescuers.

'I wonder if the fire brigade will come for us!' said Francesca. The two women giggled despite their unlikely friendship. Toonan hoped that the rescuer would bring them McDonald's, like on the advert, and Francesca wondered how long her bladder could hold out. They established that Toonan's job was a new job and she used to be 'long term unemployed' and that Francesca was a set designer for performing arts venues around the region, thus explaining the cardboard fairies.

'Have you got a boyfriend, Toonan?'

'No, I used to be a lesbian, but I like men again now.'

'Ah, you're a people person, I could tell that when I first met you,' said Francesca.

'I went speed dating the other week, and my mum tagged along. She got fixed up with Gil Von Black.'

'No way! The local rockstar?'

'I know.'

'Did you know, he even used to play with Def Leppard?!' said Francesca.

'Innit,' said Toonan. 'And I got no one, well this bloke called Small Paul from Todmorden ticked my card, but he just drove off in his Hyundai hatchback. Mum saw him just before she started necking her rock star in public.'

'Did you not tick his card then?'

'Well, I would have… I liked him, but I didn't know, then it was too late!'

'Aww, that's a shame, maybe not meant to be then, never mind,' said Francesca.

Now, at this stage, do not forget that Toonan had not visited Curmudgeon Avenue for quite some time. The last time she saw Mr Matteo Dubois was when he knocked on the door looking for his mother, Genevieve. And as for Francesca, she knew nothing of Curmudgeon Avenue and hardly knew Genevieve, despite her long term relationship with Mr Matteo Dubois. Yes, that's right... The ex-boyfriend Francesca was talking of earlier was none other than our tall, handsome and smartly dressed male with the well fancy car, Matteo Dubois. What a moment of serendipity that Francesca and Toonan should end up stuck in a lift together, waiting for their would-be rescuer.

'Oh my God, that's well tight,' Toonan said, having just heard the long story from Francesca about Matteo and his own adopted mother.

'I know, the worst thing about him was the secrets. He always had silly little secrets.'

'What like other women?'

'No, nothing like that. It was stupid, really... Matteo would even lie about what filling he had in his sandwich, little things like that.'

'Why?'

'Matteo told me he thought his mother was a liar once when he was drunk, and then when I asked him about it the next day, he said he didn't know what I was talking about.'

'Oh, I hate it when people do things like that,' Toonan spoke like the voice of reason.

'I know, maybe it was the way he had been brought up, so I just used to shrug the lies off. Then when Matteo told me he had got rid of her, I panicked at first. I thought he had killed her, but he just meant that she had offered to pay him some money to compensate him for not knowing who his real parents were. He said he would not accept it, but I later found out that he did accept it. I don't know why he lied; it wasn't even that much money. Oh, Toonan, it's a long story. I think she kidnapped him as a baby. Anyway, apparently, she moved to France, and that was the last we saw of her.'

It was at this point in the conversation that Toonan was starting to be reminded of Edna from Curmudgeon Avenue. She had allegedly moved to France.

'OMG! Right, I remember being at a party…' Toonan then proceeded to tell Francesca the whole story about Edith's birthday party and how Edna ruined it… Saying her and her French piece were moving to France. Then a bloke turns up, and that everyone thought he was a fraud investigator at first, but then he knocked on the door one day when she was visiting Harold and Edith. He said that he was looking for his mother. He said her name was summat like Guillaume, summat French-sounding, Gen something.'

'Genevieve!' said Francesca all wide eyes again. 'Genevieve Dubois?'

'That's it, yeah,' said Toonan. 'Hang on, though, that was only six months ago. When did you split up?'

'Getting on for a year ago now,' deflated Francesca.

'Oh, it's probably not the same bloke, although that would explain why he was feeling lonely,' Toonan said (I do hope she does not tell Francesca about the sex talk and the stalker theory).

'Oh, we didn't split after he got that money off his mother. I forgave him because it must've been like childhood trauma to him. But after several years of him promising to marry me, there was always some excuse, some reason he couldn't commit.'

'Oh, a commitment-phobe.'

'Yes,'

'It's a good thing it's not the same bloke though because I thought he was stalking me at one point,' said Toonan.

'Oh... dear,' Francesca thought this unlikely.

'It's my voice... I used to work the sex chat lines before cleaning toilets.'

'Oh!' (Can't blame Francesca for not knowing what to say).

'Aww, what about the real version of your bloke then?'

'Well, we sort of keep in touch; I let him face time Shelley a couple of times a week.'

'Aww, you didn't say you've got kids.'

'I don't; Shelley is a dog. If I had my phone, I'd show you a picture.'

'Nice one,' said Toonan.

Just then, the two women heard the distant voice of Elsie.

'It's just round this corner, love,' Elsie said to the lift maintenance man. She stood on her tiptoes and shouted through the little crack in the door. 'Maintenance man is here, girls, don't worry.'

As the man looked into the lift shaft, his eyes met Toonan's and hers his, with an instant flush of recognition.

'Toonan?'

'Small Paul?!' Toonan gasped and clutched Francesca by the hand (all toilet cleaning issues were now forgotten. 'It's Small Paul from Todmorden! Come to rescue us!'

Aww, well, Toonan did not mind that Small Paul had not brought McDonald's with him. All Francesca cared about was using the (freshly cleaned) toilet.

'Toonan, let me give you my phone number. Let's keep in touch... If you still see your friends from Curmudgeon Avenue, I would like to find out if this man you're talking about is the same Matteo as my Matteo,' Francesca said.

'Yeah, no worries, my sister is trying to get back with Ricky as it goes. It's his mum's house.'

'You don't mind?'

'No, why would I?'

'The sex talk!' Francesca whispered.

'Oh, no. I don't mind if you don't mind.'

The lift started making some noises and then moved to the floor that it was supposed to be on.

'Thank f*** for that!' Toonan said, greeted by the blushing face of Small Paul from Todmorden. Francesca went to use the facilities.

'Don't suppose you fancy going to McDonald's? It's time for my lunch break now,' said Small Paul. Toonan looked at Elsie for permission, who nodded her approval.

CHAPTER 19: ROCAMADOUR LOOMS.

Edna jumped out of bed and dramatically opened the blinds, allowing sunlight to bathe the room and blind a squinting Genevieve.

'Today is our visit to Rocamadour! I'm so excited!' Edna clapped her hands together and ran off to the toilet. While Genevieve listened to Edna's windy morning ablutions, she desperately tried to invent an excuse for herself. The place would be full of tourists, yes, but what if a local recognised her? Even with her hornet induced black eye... Rocamadour was a close knit community, and people had missed the foie gras expert, Eric. They missed his elusive lady friend less but still wanted to see her to find out what really happened the night he died. And only one person knew the answer to that.

'Oh, beautiful day, beautiful life partner,' Edna

clutched Genevieve's face with both hands. She kissed her on the forehead (she was going to go for the mouth, but Genevieve had not cleaned her teeth yet, and the garlic fumes were mighty). 'Time for coffee and French toast before I get to take my beautiful Genevieve to the most romantic place in the whole of France. If not the whole world! Now don't forget. French toast. Chop chop!'

'Peasant food,' Genevieve whispered to herself and flopped back into bed.

....

'Bonjour!' Edna greeted Diane and Jackson as they prepared their bulk of day trip paraphernalia.

'Ah, hello Edna, you can never be too prepared for a day out in France!' said Diane.

'Where's your wee friend?' said Jackson. 'We were hoping she could do the translations for us today. They're very French in Rocamadour.'

'Ah, here she is now,' said Edna. Genevieve entered the scene with a half-hearted effort of getting ready. Ready and disguised. A baggy jumper slipped off one shoulder, she wore sunglasses indoors, and a beret covered her entire head of hair.

'Ah well, don't you look the part! I was just saying to Edna, we need you more than ever today to translate French for us,' Jackson said.

Genevieve clutched her throat with her spiky fingers. 'I'm afraid I need to rest my voice. I 'ave a sore throat,' Genevieve croaked.

'Ohhhh,' Diane sang. 'I've just the thing here for you, some honey. I got it out for Edna's French toast, but it'll work just fine on your throat.'

'Merci,' Genevieve croaked. She took a good blob of the honey on a spoon and ladled it into her mouth. The fragrant taste induced a downturned disappointment on her lips.

'It's a bit much in one go, isn't it? Maybe I'll pour you a wee dram of whisky to wash it down with.'

'Och, Jackson, it's 10am in the morning!' said Diane.

'Aye, but it's seven in the evening somewhere,' chuckled Jackson. 'Isn't that right, Genevieve?' he elbowed Genevieve's upper arm, instigating a coughing fit. She downed the tumbler of neat whisky almost in the same fashion that a person from Manchester would. The firewater gushed down her gullet and gave her an idea. Genevieve lunged forwards, her insides now engaged in loud gastric orchestrations and made her way to the nearest bathroom.

'Blimey! Do you think she'll be alright? Only, we're almost ready to go now,' Diane nodded at Jackson, who was hurriedly rearranging their car boot so that a dining room chair could fit in. You just never know what you are going to need on a day trip.

Genevieve returned from the bathroom after several more quick successions of retching noises. 'Desole mon amie,' she clutched Edna's hand and kissed it. 'I do not think it is a good idea for me to come with you today. I am sorry.'

'You sure? We've got sick bags in the car,' Diane gestured with her thumb. Genevieve sat down.

'I think the journey may upset my predicament further, you go,' Genevieve wafted Edna away. 'Enjoy yourselves, I will be 'ere, waiting.' (Such a drama queen).

'What's this? You not coming?' Jackson said. 'That's a shame. Oh, what about the translations then?'

Genevieve opened one of her sunglasses hidden eyes. 'You two are too Scottish's for the French; just speak with a French accent, you'll be fine,' Genevieve said, and then her head flopped back on to the chair, both her arms resting on the upholstery.

CHAPTER 20: EDITH PREPARES HERSELF FOR THE ROLE OF GRANDMOTHER.

'It's definitely down there, Harold!' Edith shouted down the cellar stairs of Number One Curmudgeon Avenue (no one ever usually goes down there, as you know). 'Blue it is. Bright blue.'

Out of the darkness, Harold's face gradually became visible, his search had been fruitless, yet he was covered in dust. 'I can't see anything, Edith, nothing at all.'

'Could you just have another look, I think… try on the right-hand side,' Edith pleaded as Harold made his way back down the cellar stairs. 'Do you want me to come down there?'

'No, Edith, you leave it to Harold.'

'What? Like when we took that dog for a walk the other day at the animal sanctuary? Leave it to Harold, you said. I've never been so embarrassed in all my life,' Edith half mumbled to herself.

'The dog handler described it as a very calm dog. Docile, I think was the word they used,' said Harold.

'I can't believe you got us banned from an animal sanctuary,' Edith was obviously going to go on for longer than was reasonably necessary.

'It was the dog's fault! Never mind that Edith, I still can't see down here...'

'Have you turned the light on?' Edith shouted.

'Yeeeees,' Harold rolled his eyes. 'Bulb's covered in dust, so it's not very bright.'

'What?' Edith said. This went on for quite some time. Harold would always pretend he was a strange houseguest in situations like this. *'Where are the spare light bulbs?'* He would look confused and start rifling through cupboards. *'Do you have any bin liners, Edith?'* He would say. Harold! You have lived here at Number One Curmudgeon Avenue for longer than is reasonably necessary. Edith is not allowed to go shopping on her own, not unless you send her out at night to the off-licence. So Harold would know of any recently acquired light bulbs or bin liners because he went to the shop for them!

Harold tried his best to get out of Edith's most recent do-it-yourself task. All Edith wanted was for Harold to try and locate the cot that had belonged to baby Ricky Ricketts all those years ago. Saved by the hopeful and proud grandparents, Mr and Mrs Payne, who at the time expected an abundance of grandchildren. But it was not to be, as you know, Ricky Ricketts was an only child. And Edna was not about to ruin her life by having a baby - too selfish, and it was not as though she could have convinced a man to impregnate her.

Harold continued to rummage around, and Edith could hear him making victory type noises; maybe he has found it? Then she heard him, one foot after the other, scraping his way back upstairs.

'Did you find it then? Where is it? Is it too heavy for you?' Edith did Harold's head in with her multiple question-asking, here comes another one; 'What's that under your arm?'

'Nothing,' said Harold, shoving the rectangular-shaped, magazine-sized object further away from Edith's prying eyes. 'Nothing at all!'

'I can see something! And it isn't Ricky's cot!'

Now, do you remember the rucksack incident? Edith still had those armpit tickling skills, which she held on to for moments like this.

'Ow, geroff!' Harold said, but it was no good; he had let go of his exciting find. Edith looked inside the brown A4 sized envelope with pursed lips.

'Oh, it's just one of Edna's paintings! Nothing to get excited about... did you think you had just stumbled on a valuable masterpiece?'

'No, no, I told you it was nothing at all, but you bullied me into showing you!' well done, Harold.

'Right, I'm going down there,' Edith rolled her sleeves up. 'Honestly, want something doing, do it yourself.' Pushing past Harold, Edith stomped down the stairs, located the *correct* light switch, and the cellar flooded with light. And then went a bit darker as the door slammed behind Harold. 'What are you doing?'

'I don't know? Following you, to help you upstairs with the cot!' Harold said. 'And where was that light switch? Hmm? See, this was your parent's house, Edith you can't expect me to know...'

But Harold's voice trailed off because Edith could see deeper into the cellar in the improved light situation. She had found Ricky's cot! Now, do you remember those bright blue resin bathroom suites popular in the nineteen-seventies? After a few years of wear and tear and a bit of abrasive scrubbing, they became a sickly sort of turquoise colour? If you don't remember those bathrooms, try and imagine it because this was the colour of Ricky Ricketts' old cot. Edith gasped; she ran her fingers along the top rail. The mattress inside the cot frame was old, grey and saggy. Both Harold and Edith looked down at the sorry sight.

'Oh Edith, I don't think they'll want it,' said Harold.

'What do you mean? A new coat of paint and new mattress, new bedding it'll be fine Harold, don't be such a… a down in the mouth.' Edith started dragging the cot towards the staircase. Harold had no choice but to comply.

'What if the baby's a girl?' Harold could not help himself.

'Paint it pink then,' Edith had stopped halfway up the staircase… 'Unless.'

'Unless? Come on, Edith, keep going, almost at the top now.'

'Well, what about Wantha? She was clearly pregnant, which means I'm going to have two grandchildren.'

'Wantha was clearly ignoring us… Maybe it's someone else's baby?' There you go again, Harold, taking the jam out of Edith's doughnut.

'Oh, Harold,' Edith exasperated.

'Don't bring me into it… your Ricky can't control himself. If it's true that he's got two women pregnant at the same time, he should have told us!

We never got to the bottom of it the other day!'

'Maybe we shouldn't have run away and hidden in the bedroom?'

'I know,' said Harold.

'I was worried about getting to know Gemma. She seemed a bit hoity-toity for us, Harold.'

'Speak for yourself, Edith. I'm a reader of newspapers, and she's a journalist.'

'Well, anyway, she invited me to come with her for her scan today. I'm so excited; I get to see my very first grandchild. That's what got me on to looking for the cot... oh, today! I'd better get ready! Oh, I've reached the top!' Edith let go of the cot and started fiddling with the cellar door handle.

'Edith! I can't hold it; it's heavier than it looks!' Harold, who was weaker than he looks, struggled to keep hold of the other end of the cot, while Edith struggled to open the door.

'It won't open!' she rattled the door handle. 'It won't open, Harold. We're trapped!'

To make the situation worse, Edith completely let go of the cot, which fell down the cellar staircase, taking Harold with it and smashed noisily into about one thousand splintery pieces.

CHAPTER 21: GENEVIEVE FRENCHES IT UP.

Genevieve was careful, making sure that the Bove's car was out of sight. She even left a little time for them to return to the Chateau le Grincheaux on a forgotten umbrella mission, which they did not. Then Genevieve whipped off her beret, stripped herself of her big baggy jumper, replaced her sunglasses and slinked off to the terrace area with a packet of cigarettes wedged in her bikini bottoms, a box of Diane's chocolates in one hand and Jackson's whisky bottle in the other. It was now ten in the morning, and the terrace area was bathed in sunlight. Genevieve pulled one of the sun loungers to the very sunniest position and arranged her lone party around herself. Chocolates, a bottle of whisky (no need for a glass), she started swigging out of the bottle. Sacre bleu! She said to herself, having forgotten her lighter. Ah! Ooo, is siz coming up the driveway? Genevieve struck a pose on that sun lounger and peeped over the top of her sunglasses.

'Bonjour Madame,' said a young and hunky looking builder wearing a sleeveless vest.

'Oiselle, Mademoiselle!' Genevieve corrected, laughed and twirled her finger around her hair. She removed one cigarette and positioned it to her pouting lips. 'Got a light, Monsieur?'

'Non... Madam... oiselle I do not smoke.'

'Oh, never mind,' Genevieve disappointed.

'Is Madame Bove at 'ome?'

'Erm... non! Sey arrr out for zee day,' Genevieve pouted. Having Frenched it up, she looked into the van and spied another young male. Her left eyebrow lifted behind her sunglasses.

'We have come to fix the holes in the chimney,' the young man spoke in French. Genevieve picked up the word 'fix'.

'Pardon Monsieur, I am a little hard of 'earing,' Genevieve pouted.

'Never mind, we don't need to get into the house. We can get on with it and bill Mr and Mrs Bove later.'

Genevieve looked at both the men blankly but continued to pout, pose, and rearrange her sunglasses. The silence had been going on for quite some time. Genevieve turned around and completed what she thought was a sexy walk back to the sun lounger. The two builders shrugged at one another, got out of their van and started unloading their ladders and tools.

Suit yourself, thought Genevieve as she made her way back to her (melting) chocolates and whisky bottle.

Meanwhile, the day-trippers had arrived at their destination.

'Oh wait until you see this little street and all its shops, Edna, you'll love it,' Diane said. Jackson parked the car, and Edna took in the expanse of the towering cliff, medieval buildings cascaded down the side, and a line of steps, like rock coloured tinsel. Edna felt breathless just at the sight of it. Maybe Genevieve really was avoiding Rocamadour with her coughing fit. The further Edna walked up that hillside, with its buildings that seemed to beautifully tumble down one after the other, the easier it became. It was the strangest thing. Swept up in the magical beauty of the pilgrimage place, Edna's footsteps became as light as air, her loose-fitting maxi dress fluttered in the breeze. They reached the location that Jackson had identified as the most romantic location in Rocamadour. The cafe at the top of the hill. Edna was keen to grab a seat. The view was stunning. Diane beamed at her with silent satisfaction. They both sighed because soon, they would be sipping wine. Jackson was busy taking photographs of circling ravens soaring with spread wings sailing along in the blue, blue sky.

'Oh, I feel as light as air!' Edna said.

'Blimey, you've not even had a glass of wine yet.'

'Oh, yes! Let's order some wine!' said Diane, pretending this was not the first thing on her mind.

'Haha, brilliant! I'll have to carry you two down the hill, as well as drive you home!' said Jackson.

'Don't worry, Jackson, you've got that bottle of whisky for later!' Edna said. She was really getting the hang of this happiness thing.

Back at the chateau, Genevieve and Jackson's aforementioned bottle of whisky kept each other company on the sun terrace. Today was the hottest day in France so far that year. The builders had almost finished patching up the holes in all the chimneys (no more smoke billowing out of the sides in winter). It was almost time to climb down the ladders, but one of them spotted something on the sun terrace and nudged his workmate. It was the sight of Madame Genevieve Dubois, bare-breasted like two aspirins on an ironing board. She lowered her sunglasses slightly, very slightly and observed her targets, both observing her from their place of work at the top of the castle. *Ooo,* Genevieve said to herself. She fondled her own sexagenarian epidermis with factor zero sun oil. Genevieve tried to position herself without covering her body, enabling her to sip more whisky. But wouldn't you know it; she slipped right off that sun lounger and landed in Diane's melted sheet of chocolates.

'Merde!' Genevieve said. The two strapping builders were at her side a bit too quickly for her liking, despite her earlier teasing.

'Pardon, Mademoiselle,' the first builder said. He gestured to his colleague, who tried to avert his eyes while offering Genevieve her own happy coat.

'Are you alright!?' he raised his voice because Genevieve told them she was slightly deaf in her earlier performance.

'Merci,' Genevieve managed. Her knees were covered in chocolate, and her sunglasses had travelled west. She accepted her garment, which on covering her body, stuck to her limbs like cling film on cheap ham. Genevieve, despite her date with the terrace flags, was able to work her magic, adjusting her posture and sunglasses; she recovered the almost empty whisky bottle.

'Join me?' she said.

The two men looked at one another and nodded in French agreement.

Meanwhile, in Rocamadour, the ravens had gone to roost, and the wine flowed. Jackson had gone to look at some of what he called 'religious buildings'. Edna was feeling a little guilty for enjoying herself so much without Genevieve. She was not to know that her lover was having a party of her own back at the chateau.

'So how did you and Genevieve first meet then?' Diane said.

'Well,' Edna started. 'I was an artist at the time...' (HA!) 'Genevieve and her adopted son moved into the duplex flat next door...' Edna was tipsy, the effects of which was that her speech folded into a drunken poshness.

'Oh, she has a son?!' Diane scraped her chair a little nearer.

'Well,' Edna eyed her companion. 'Between yourself, myself and the Bordeaux,' (she lifted her wine glass at this point, spilling a little from it). 'She doesn't like to talk about him. He tried to sue her because he had no adoption certificate. You see, this meant he couldn't get a passport, and this meant he couldn't wed his fiancée.'

'Well, that doesn't sound right,' said a frowning Diane.

'It's true,' said Edna. 'Oh, I've already said too

much. You don't want to hear of how Genevieve's villainous son conned her out of thousands and thousands of pounds.'

'No. I meant it doesn't sound right about the certificate and the passports. Say, for example, you lose your birth certificate; there are ways of getting a replacement. Same I imagine if you're adopted.'

'No, it's true,' Edna looked around to make sure no one was watching. 'The French, I imagine they are not as reliable with their paperwork as the British.' (Steady on, Edna, that's a bit of a sweeping generalisation).

'No, but to sue his own adopted mother!' Diane tutted.

'They settled out of court in the end. We had to take a loan out against my bungalow,' Edna gulped down her wine, blackening her teeth in the process. 'Then, of course, poor Genevieve fled, returned here to France.'

'What, here, here in Rocamadour? I'm surprised she didn't want to come today!' said Diane.

'She couldn't come; she was unwell, remember,' Edna was quick to answer. 'Anyway, she moved about, I understand. We lost touch, to be honest.' Edna observed Diane's face, a picture of pity. 'Then she turned up, out of the blue, my parents had died, and I had moved back into their house. Genevieve tracked me down, couldn't keep away in the end, so it seemed, despite the heartbreak over her adopted son.'

'Oh, how romantic!' said Diane. 'I love stories about couples getting back together, two souls that cannot live without each other. Did you ever see that episode of *Sex and the City*? The one where Miranda asked Steve to meet her on the bridge if they had decided to stay together?'

'No,' said Edna, (can't see her watching that, can you?)

'Anyway,' Edna crashed her wine glass on to the table a bit more forcefully than she had intended. 'Enough about you...'

'Hey?' Diane said.

'I mean, enough about ME, how did you and Jackson meet?'

'Oh, same thing really, he moved in next door with his adopted son, had to leave the country for an extended period of time, but returned because he couldn't live without me...' said Diane.

'REALLY?' Edna gushed.

'No! Ha! I'm joking!' Diane put her hand on Edna's forearm to prove her well-meant tease. 'Nothing as exciting as you two; we just met at work. We have a grown-up son and daughter, and we both took early retirement after falling in love with the chateau life.'

'Oh, lovely,' Edna smiled her smile, decorated

with her red wine moustache.

'Oh, here he is now, have you completed your pilgrimage, husband?' Diane said as Jackson got to the top of the steps and entered the cafe.

'Aye, and wait till I show you what I've found pinned to a wall!' Jackson got his mobile out of his pocket and sat down. 'Who do you think this looks like?' he was laughing now. 'We'll have to show her when we get back; she'll have a right laugh!' Jackson showed Diane and Edna the photograph he took of a poster of a woman with French writing. Diane squinted her eyes.

'Who? Who is it supposed to look like?' Diane said. 'Oh, I know, is it Joanna Lumley?'

Edna took the phone out of Diane's hands, Jackson was still grinning. 'No, not Joanna Lumley... let Edna have a good look.'

Edna had a good look, and looking back at her, even though it was a photograph of a photograph, there was no doubt about it, was a blonde version of Genevieve. There was no mistaking it. 'Oh, that looks just like Genevieve, oh, she's never been blonde, though! And what does this writing mean?' Edna attempted to get the attention of a passing waitress. 'Scooosee,' she said (well, Genevieve did tell her to put on a French accent) 'Parlez-vous Francais?' Edna immediately realised her mistake. 'Oh hahaha! Pardon, parlez-vous English?!'

Jackson raised his eyebrow at Edna's 'Brit's abroad' French, and Diane gestured with her forefinger and thumb that Edna was sloshed.

'Ah, Oui madam, 'ow can I help you?' the waitress was used to this kind of tourist nonsense.

'What does this writing say on this poster?'

The waitress did not need to squint her eyes or read the writing. 'Ah, it says THE BLACK WIDOW OF ROCAMADOUR. It is a wanted poster... A very famous news story around here a couple of years ago. The foie gras seller died in suspicious circumstances, and his lady friend did a buuunk,' she shrugged.

'Oh! Well, it's definitely not Genevieve then!' Edna said.

'I can't remember the woman's name, but I sink it was a British name,' said the waitress, Jackson tipped her, and the three of them sighed and laughed. 'Oh, and rumour has it, she moved to Paris and bumped off another one!'

'Oh, that's so funny! Oh wait until I show Genevieve, oh, they do say that everyone has a dongle,' said Edna.

'Do you mean a doppelganger?'

'Yes, that's it hahaha, oh my goodness! This French wine is rather potent, isn't it?' said Edna.

'Aye, it is, especially if you drink three bottles of the stuff in one afternoon,' said Diane.

'Ahh, daytime drinking… well, cheers to that! Let's head back,' said the sober Jackson.

Well, as you can imagine, Edna slept soundly in the back of Mr and Mrs Bove's car on the way back to Chateau le Grincheaux. All those steps, all that wine, it was understandable. Even the sound of tyres on the gravel path did not wake her. But the sound of their return alerted another pair of drunken ears… Her building buddies long gone, Genevieve in a two-piece, leapt off the sun lounger. She expertly disguised herself as 'ill Genevieve'. She kicked the empty bottle of whisky under the bushes but then thought better of it. Jackson *had* encouraged her to drink some to make her feel better.

'Oh bonjour, bonjour! I 'ave missed you!' Genevieve croaked, maintaining the illusion of illness. 'Your builders have attended to your chimneys while you have been away. I offered them a whisky as I 'ad no Euros to offer. 'Ope you don't mind, Meester Bove'

A disappointed Jackson took the empty bottle from his French lodger. 'Nay bother,' he gritted his teeth and then noticed the empty chocolate box under the sun lounger. What is this woman playing at? Diane was busily trying to rouse drunk Edna, now hung-over Edna, who brightened when she saw Genevieve.

'Oh! Genevieve, wait until I show you this... Mr Bove, did you forward me that photo?' she said, scrambling around in her handbag. 'Ah, yes, wait until I show you this photograph we found; it looks just like you! But on a *wanted* poster!'...

CHAPTER 22: MR AND MRS BOVE ARE GLAD THAT THEY DID NOT HAVE THE SPY HOLE FILLED IN.

'What did you make of all that then?' Jackson said to Diane as they settled down alone for the evening. Their two drunken guests had sloped off to bed without getting undressed. The chateau owners compared notes of the information they had gleaned about the pair. Jackson opted not to tell Diane that he had spotted the empty box of her chocolates.

'When we first met them, on first impressions, I just thought them an odd couple, you know an odd pairing. I've got to know Edna a little better today. All that posh talk is just an act, you know,' Diane said.

'Are you saying you want to befriend the woman?' said Jackson.

'Oh, I wouldn't go that far! And anyway, the more I find out about Genevieve, I'll be hoping they don't want to come back next year,' said Diane.

'So she was missing, living in France for around ten years then?' Jackson asked.

'Yes, so she could have changed her hair colour.'

'What! Do you really think it was her on that poster?'

'Yes, I do, and what's more is that cock-and-bull story about having to settle out of court with her adopted son, sounds like she has already taken Edna for a ride,' said Diane.

'Oh, my goodness! Are you thinking what I'm thinking?' Jackson sat up in bed.

'Aye, husband I am, if Genevieve bumped off her lovers, then returned to Edna, to hide in Manchester, is she now going to bump off Edna?!... In our chateau!' Diane understandably had got carried away, but then so had Jackson.

'I didn't think that. I thought it's a good job we weren't at home when the builders came today, we would have asked them to block up that spy hole, and we'll be needing that more than ever now. A woman's life is at stake!'

Mr and Mrs Bove crept down their corridor until they reached their false cupboard door. They both had a listen, but all they could hear was Genevieve coughing in her sleep and Edna snoring and farting in hers, all of which was alcohol-fuelled. 'I think she's safe for the time being,' said Jackson.

Later that same night, Edna woke up. The fumes in their bedroom were enough to make anyone have a coughing fit, even Smoky Mc Smoke-Face Genevieve. Edna went to the bathroom. As she sat there, the moonlight shone through the open bathroom door illuminating the sleeping Genevieve's brunette hair. Yes, she would look like Joanna Lumley if she had fairer hair. But no! Edna immediately felt guilty for thinking the poster really was a photograph of Genevieve. What had that waitress said? It was a British name? Oh must have been a look-alike, or perhaps it actually was Joanna Lumley! Enough of these silly thoughts, Edna returned to bed but could not resist another look at the photograph. Had Jackson forwarded it to her phone? He said he would... ahh, yes, there it is. Edna messed around with her Smartphone while lying down, and in the haze of hung-over brain fog, accidentally posted the image to Instagram.

Meanwhile, in Whitefield, Wantha Rose was the proud owner of a new mobile phone. She had spent the best part of the day engaged in her own personal fashion show. Wantha was all made up with nowhere to go. Except for appearing in several thousand selfies in cyberspace, mostly for Ricky Ricketts' benefit. Wantha was alone in the house, on account of Toonan going on a date with Small Paul from Todmorden, and Patchouli had more or less moved in with Gil Von Black. Wantha's phone made a noise. The same noise a new Smartphone would make when its new owner had not quite figured out how to turn off the notifications for each and every social media platform... Especially Instagram. Wantha struggled to see clearly at first, her right eye slightly glued together with cheap fake eyelash glue. After dismissing the disappointment that Ricky Ricketts had not noticed her earlier efforts, Wantha *noticed* the notification '*Edna Payne has posted for the first time in a while*'. Spinster sisters? Wantha said to herself, her gel nail manicured finger struggling to scroll upwards on the phone screen. There it was, Edna's post. No caption, just a photograph of a photograph surrounded by some French writing. If Wantha had paid attention in her Castlebrook high school French lesson, she would have been able to read: 'WANTED BY FRENCH POLICE'. There was another row of writing, presumably the miscreant's name, but this had been cropped by social media posting conventions. Wantha peeled off her fake eyelash and had another look.

'WTF has Edna posted a photo of Joanna Lumley on Instagram?' Wantha said to herself. She flopped back on her bed but could not resist having another look at Ricky Ricketts' Facebook. (Having previously unfriended him, she now had to use Toonan's login details). Wantha thought nothing because Ricky had not shared his employment status for the public to admire. The benefits agency may be watching (and Matteo Dubois had sworn him to secrecy). Ricky had not updated his relationship status either. This gave Wantha a flutter of hope. If Ricky had been serious about Gemma Hampsons and her authentic baby bump, surely he would have been bragging about it on Facebook? Wantha noticed a message from her sister at the top of the screen.

'WOTCHA SIS. HAROLD AND EDIFF HAVE INVITED US ROUND. MUM BUMPED INTO THEM IN MORRISONS AND INVITED HERSELF AND HER FANCY PIECE.'

'Hah!' Wantha gasped to herself. She typed out several messages and then deleted them. They all involved '*Having to see if she was free*' but what on earth was Wantha going to do instead? Her full-time job (Patchouli) had moved out to Ringley Road to live with the real rock star, Gil Von Black. Incidentally, Ringley Road is the most sought after and well-to-do area of Whitefield (mostly built *after* Curmudgeon Avenue, you understand).

Instagram selfies only take up so much of a person's time. Wantha Rose would have no excuse not to attend the gathering, and there was the added bonus that she had been missing Edith. They all had, she hadn't missed Harold, not so much, but you could not enjoy Edith without enduring Harold. Wantha made herself comfortable again and tried to get back to sleep, expecting her sister to return home from her third date with Small Paul from Todmorden. You might as well go back to sleep, Wantha; there are developments on that front that, I must insist, are a story for a later date.

CHAPTER 23: TIFFIN!

The dubious sound emitting from Matteo Dubois' back office had continued during the entire renovation project of Number Three, Curmudgeon Avenue. The plastering had dried, and electrics had sparked. There was soon to be shop fittings, decorating and flooring. Things were all on schedule; the team of Matteo Dubois, Ricky Ricketts and Harry the Bastard were working like clockwork together. Every day, Matteo would retire to his back office at exactly the same time. Ricky rolled his eyes, and Harry frowned.

'You know, I'm not sure that's what we thought it was,' Harry said.

'Ha! Course it is! I even heard him saying a girl's name the other day when I was doing the skirting boards down there.' Ricky gestured with his paintbrush, almost flicking paint in Harry's face. 'What was it now? Sally? No Shelley, or summat like that... Shelley! Shelley! He was saying.'

'Shhh!' said Harry.

'Yes, Ricky? Did you shout to me?' Matteo popped out of his office with no visual sign of any embarrassment.

'Oh... yeah, I'm running out of paint for these skirtings. Want me to nip to the wholesalers?' (Nice save, Ricky).

'Don't worry, mate, it's on my list,' said Matteo grabbing his hoody. 'Right, see you guys in an hour or so. Want me to pick anything up while I'm out?'

'No boss, we'll be reet,' said Harry, as Matteo shut the front door and drove away in his well fancy car. The two labourers sat down in their own makeshift office, a couple of plastic garden chairs in the back yard. Ricky did what anyone would do when left alone at work; he rolled himself a fat one and lit up.

'Champion,' said Harry the Bastard, meeting his temporary work colleague and full-time friend with a cup of tea. Soon they would be putting the world to rights and coming up with some great ideas. It was not long before those big nostrils that belong to our friend Harold caught a whiff of a vaguely familiar and fun smell. Ricky noticed the top of Harold's head just over the adjoining wall. He nudged Harry and nodded at Harold. The two of them sat in silence until Harold's bristling yet sparse hair disappeared, closely followed by the familiar sound of Ricky's mother's voice...

'I can't smell anything, Harold,' Edith loudly whispered.

'Shh Edith! Reminds me of that couple we met on our honeymoon,' Harold said, and the two labourers giggled from inside Matteo's back yard.

'Ohhh, I think your right, Harold! I've smelt that smell before, on our Ricky.'

'Well, he's working next door, isn't he?' Harold said.

'Ricky! Is that you love?' Edith shouted over the wall.

The two scamps burst out laughing like a couple of naughty teenagers. Edith climbed up onto the same bench that Wantha and Mrs Ali used when spying over the wall. Harold joined her, and the bench squeaked like a weird see-saw.

'Alright, you two!' said a rather relaxed Ricky. 'What happened to you the other day? You missed Gemma's scan, made her well paranoid.'

'Oh, we got locked in the cellar. I was trying to get a surprise for you and the baby.'

'Oh yeah?' said Ricky. 'Out of the cellar?'

'Yes, Richard, your old cot,' said Edith.

'That old thing! Gemma's not gonna want that. Anyway, it's a girl. We found out at the scan.'

'A girl! Oh, A girl, oh!' Edith clutched her floral

dress in between her legs as excitement kicked in. 'Well, when where you going to tell me?'

'Err… at the scan which you didn't turn up to.'

'Oh, oh, you don't seem too bothered oh, I'm going to be a grandmother… to a girl!'

'He's not too bothered, you're right, Mrs Goatshed. I noticed that,' said Harry the Bastard (he's ever so polite, you know).

'I am! It just doesn't seem real, you know not till it arrives.'

'She arrives,' Harry said, taking in another drag of the funny fag.

'Yeah, she,' mumbled Ricky.

'Mmm, I know what you mean, your father… Sorry, Harold…' Edith turned to Harold for fear of mentioning her deceased first husband, and Harold wobbled his head with indifference. 'He was convinced you were a boy, and he painted that cot bright blue before I was even three months gone!'

'But I am… I mean, I was a boy.'

'I know,' said Edith.

'So it didn't matter,' said Ricky.

'Well, it doesn't matter because we got locked in the cellar, and the cot ended up smashed to smithereens. Sorry about that, Ricky,' said Harold.

'No worries, Harold, Gemma's loaded innit, lives on Sunnybank Road. I think she wants all the designer gear for baby, keeps telling me.'

'Oh?' said Edith.

'Designer baby?' said Harold.

'Innit,' said Ricky Ricketts.

There was silence for a few moments. Edith and Harold still perched over that back wall, Ricky and Harry finishing the funny fags. Hopefully, Matteo was still at the wholesalers. It was Ricky who broke the silence.

'Got any biscuits, Mum?'

'Always,' said Edith, jumping off her perch and opening her back gate for the naughty teenagers to enter. 'Put the kettle on, Harold. I think it's time we told Richard who we saw in Marks and Spencer the other day.'

Tea was brewed, biscuit tins were raided. Ricky and Harry made themselves comfortable.

'Ricky, I blame myself,' Harold went all head wobbling and annoying. 'When I became your step-father, I neglected to tell you about the birds and the bees.'

Harry the Bastard's ginger nut biscuit, half soaked in his tea, split into two halves, dramatically dropping into his cup.

'Eff off Harold, I was thirty-eight when you and

Mum got married!' Ricky Ricketts said.

'Very well,' said Harold, all official-like. This was well awkward for Harry the Bastard and Edith. 'The other day, the other day, RICHARD, myself and your mother spotted Wantha Rose in a state of what can only be described as the third trimester of pregnancy!' Harold's head almost wobbled right off his shoulders. Edith clutched her hand around the neckline of her floral dress, her eyes immediately pinkie-fied.

'What! ... Did she speak to you?' said Ricky.

'No, I don't think she noticed me, though I was trying to get her attention, you know I had a soft spot for her,' said Edith. Actually, this speech about how fond she was of Wantha Rose went on for longer than was reasonably necessary, but you get the gist. 'She definitely looked pregnant, though.'

'Well, look at this,' Ricky retrieved his phone from his jeans pocket. Harold and Edith both squinted to look at the various (Photoshopped) selfies of Wantha that Ricky had recovered from his Instagram account. Her stomach was flat, flat and bare. Her lips were pouted, her makeup was the envy of the entire North West of England, and her hair was glorious. Wantha Rose looked better than she had ever looked in her whole life on those photographs. You could say she was 'blooming', but she was definitely not pregnant. Ricky *had* noticed those selfies that Wantha had worked so hard over.

Ricky took his phone back off his mother. 'Mum! You've accidentally 'liked' all these photos of Wantha. Did you press that heart logo?'

'Oh, I don't know Ricky, I don't know how to work technology,' said Edith, wringing her hands together. 'I do like those pictures, though, so what's wrong with that? She looks very pretty.'

'It will look as though *I* have liked the pictures! That's what's wrong, Mum! Gemma's gonna go off her head!'

(It's a good job that Ricky had not followed his Auntie Edna on Instagram. Things will get explosive around here if these nincompoops are not careful!).

'We'd better go back next door and make it look like we've been doing some work,' said Harry the Bastard, as latent paranoia swept over him.

'Wait!' said Harold. 'Tell them about Saturday, Edith.'

'Oh, yes, we saw Patchouli and Gil Von Black in Morrisons the other day. She invited herself round on Saturday afternoon.'

'Both of them,' Harold raised his eyebrows and nodded at Ricky Ricketts and Harry the Bastard.

'That's when Gemma and me are coming round!' said Ricky.

'I know it'll be fine; we'll put a bit of food on,' said Edith. 'We'll call it Tiffin!'

Just then, Ricky Ricketts and Harry the Bastard jumped out of their skins at the sound of a well fancy car returning to Curmudgeon Avenue. 'Shit, Harry! Leg it next door!' Ricky said...

Well, at least we have Saturday afternoon to look forward to. Harold and Edith are putting on Tiffin!

CHAPTER 24: MR AND MRS BOVE ARE CONCERNED FOR EDNA'S SAFETY.

When Edna showed Genevieve the photograph of the wanted poster found on public display in Rocamadour, she had stared at it, and her face contorted into a gasp of panic. Genevieve said nothing for longer than was reasonably necessary, then tossed the phone back to Edna, pursed her lips and said: 'That… is Joanna Lumley!'

Edna, of course, tried to continue the conversation. Did Genevieve not think it was funny that a wanted poster looked just like her? Edna knew Genevieve had always been a brunette. She did not care for bleach blonde hair. Or did she? And had she definitely lived in Rocamadour? Is that why she did not go on the day out? No, she was ill... but something was bothering Edna, she was no mind reader, but Diane and Jackson had seemed a bit funny since the day out to Rocamadour. Oh, dear! Edna was filled with horror when she thought of how she had slept all the way back to the chateau. Consumed with a hungover person's guilt and deep embarrassment from admitting to herself that she may have broken wind in the back of that car. What a fool Edna felt! Of course, she was snoring and farting, but that was not what was on Mr and Mrs Bove's mind.

'I still think you should say something,' said Diane.

'Me?' Jackson's eyes were wide. 'Why does it have to be me? And anyway, what do you want me to say? I saw your picture on a wanted poster?! Edna has already asked her, she said it wasn't her, it's a photo of Joanna Lumley!'

'Ha, that's stupid. What would Joanna Lumley be doing in France?'

'I don't know, Diane, maybe she was murdering her husbands!' said Jackson, perhaps a little too loudly as Genevieve walked into the room.

'Bonjour, what are we arguing about? Can I join in? I do enjoy a lovers tiff!' Genevieve said, rather cheekily.

'Oh hahaha,' Mr and Mrs Bove laughed in unison; Jackson decided to partially fess up. 'Ahh, we were just wondering what on earth Joanna Lumley is doing in France?'

'We weren't arguing. We're just loud...' said Diane. Both the Boves laughed long and loudly.

'Oh, Edna is the same. I don't understand sis British sense of humour. She also thinks it's hilarious that there is a poster of Joanna Lumley.'

Now was Mr and Mrs Bove's chance. 'Well, it was the fact that it looks just like you...' said Jackson.

'Tsk,' Genevieve batted the situation away.

'Well, don't you think it's funny?' said Diane.

'Non, I 'ave no opinion, either way. It is not me, so it's not funny, maybe we just 'ave different sense of fun,' Genevieve swished her dress and self away to her favourite place, the sun terrace.

'The cheek of it!' whispered Jackson.

'I don't know about you, but I think they've, well, Genevieve has outstayed her welcome,' said Diane. Mr and Mrs Bove glanced out of the window, they could not be sure, but Genevieve appeared to be giving them the death stare behind her sunglasses.

'Where is Edna? You go and ask,' said Diane to her husband.

'Me again? Why me!?' Jackson put down his coffee mug but decided against approaching Genevieve, there was no need, as their other house guest arrived in the room.

'Ah, I see Genevieve has told you we're thinking of going to Paris for a few days?' breezed Edna. Diane and Jackson looked at one another in a '*what now*' kind of expression. 'Don't worry, I will pay you for the days we're absent.'

'That won't be necessary,' laughed Diane, while Jackson spoke at the same time; 'That's very good of you, Edna, thank you.'

Edna's nose reached the ceiling, her mouth smiled at the same time, which, as you know, was unusual for her.

'Actually, Edna, Genevieve did not mention Paris. We wanted to ask her about that wanted poster,' Diane said. (Don't forget, while this is going on, Genevieve has fixed her stare from outside inwards, despite being hidden behind large dark sunglasses).

'Oh, ha, oh!' said Edna, her nose now where it should be. 'She just didn't find it amusing that we thought she looked like Joanna Lumley. I do think the French have a slightly different yet significant sense of humour, you know.'

'Forget Joanna Lumley; we wanted to know if it's really her on that photo!' Diane said in hushed tones while sneaking a glance at the stick-thin death stare.

Edna laughed her best fake laugh, 'Oh, oh no, my dear, Genevieve would *never* bleach her hair blonde.'

'Aye, but would she bump off her husband?' Jackson took it too far, and Diane shot him her own death stare. 'Sorry, Edna, only pulling your leg.'

'Anyway, as I was saying, myself and Genevieve are due to visit Paris this weekend,' Edna resumed her self-righteous posture. 'And may I remind you, Mr Bove, that Genevieve and myself are… well, she is not the type of women to have a husband!' Edna shushed the latter part of her sentence. Genevieve must be able to lip read or something because she hid behind her newspaper and tried to conceal a giggling fit. Edna swished herself out of the French doors and onto the sun terrace, where she joined Genevieve with a kiss on her forehead. They held hands as Edna sat down onto the (now sagging) sun lounger.

'Paris, my arse,' said Jackson, which was followed by a screeching and loud laugh from the garden area.

'Say nothing,' pleaded his wife.

CHAPTER 25: THE AMBIVALENT WELCOME

'Leave it to Harold, he said,' Edith was talking to herself in the front room. 'It will be fine, he said.' She was angrily puffing out those dust-covered pillows. Everything looks dusty in everyone's front room on a sunny day, don't worry, Edith. Although they had ample opportunity to get the shopping in for their in-between meals event this Saturday, Harold, being Harold, had decided to take control of the organisation… What Edith had said was correct, '*Leave it to Harold*' he had said…

And now Saturday was here, Harold insisted to Edith that the hoovering and mopping of floors *'didn't need doing'.* He was going out shopping without her, as he wanted to go right then. He did not give Edith time to have a shower. She was still in a state of undress while Harold was out at the supermarket. Having taken the bins out, made the beds (a bit excessive Edith, your guests aren't staying over). Edith disobediently mopped and hoovered the floors and set to work on the lengthy task of dusting the various knick-knacks and nonsense scattered around Curmudgeon Avenue. All she had to do was put the laundry away but decided against this as she was running out of time - which was all Harold's fault.

What was Ricky's new and pregnant girlfriend going to think of her boyfriend and baby daddy's mother? After hiding the laundry under the stairs, Edith retreated to her bedroom, where she would commence operation Edith, in an attempt to make herself look as endearing as possible to her new potential daughter-in-law. She looked at herself in the mirror and sighed a baggy sigh. Edith missed Wantha if she was honest (so do I, but don't worry Edith, you'll be seeing her in a bit, you don't know it yet, but she's coming round). Edith reached for her moisturiser cream and unscrewed the lid. She heard a rattling sound, which vanished, and then, a few minutes later, the front doorbell knocker banged. Oh, for goodness sake! I don't get a minute to myself; I hope it's not any of the guests. I haven't finished getting ready yet. Edith travelled barefoot down the staircase; the rubbing in of her moisturiser and grumbling lasted until she reached the front door.

'Harold!' Edith gasped as she turned to return

upstairs in a hurry. 'Why did you knock on the door? You live here!'

'Forgot my key, and you've locked the back door.'

'Well, I was about to get undressed and have a shower!'

'You knew it was only me coming home from the shop.'

'Well, why didn't you take your key? Idiot.' Edith spoke her last word under her breath.

Their bickering lasted all the way upstairs. Harold had dumped all the shopping at the bottom of the stairs. When they reached the bathroom, there was a standoff.

'You're not going in there! I need a shower!'

'I'm bursting!' said Harold, pushing; yes, pushing Edith out of the way. 'You look fine as you are.' Harold shut the door in Edith's face.

'Oh, well, hurry up Harold, they'll be here in a bit, and I've still got my nightdress on!' shouted Edith through the door. You should know, Edith, that these things cannot be rushed, not with Harold, especially not with Harold. Edith went downstairs to check and unpack the shopping. Her journey down the staircase was accompanied by the sound of Harold dropping the kids off at the pool. Harold could not be trusted to execute the shopping list without going off-script. Edith noticed he had taken his rucksack with him and raised an eyebrow. Harold was still straining upstairs by the sounds of it, so she decided to leave the rucksack until last, give her husband a chance…

Meanwhile, on the Hillock estate;

'You look nice,' said Patchouli when she entered her former home. She had not moved out officially but had not stayed there for weeks and weeks.

'Alright,' Wantha addressed her mother with dull tones. She looked at Gil Von Black, standing behind Patchouli in the doorway. As the two women crossed paths, Wantha made that clicking sound she does with her tongue and the roof of her mouth and turned her back on Gil.

'Are you ready then, love? Only Gil doesn't want to leave his car outside…' Patchouli said.

'OH! Go without me den… Wantha Rose will walk all the way to Curmudgeon Avenue on her own.' (Oooh! Watch out, Patchouli! Your daughter is talking about herself in the third person!)

'No worries, we can wait, honestly,' Gil Von Black was slightly amused by this mother and daughter exchange. 'We're early.'

'See,' said Wantha, throwing her poor mother a look. 'I just need to find my lip liner, innit.'

Patchouli observed the image of her daughter. 'Are you anxious about going to Curmudgeon Avenue in case you see Ricky Ricketts?'

'Who?' Wantha batted her eyelids at her mother.

'What do you mean who? He might not even be there.'

'Do not...' Wantha orchestrated with her makeup brush. 'Come to me with any chit-chat about that boi, Mother.'

'Shall I go and wait in the car?' Gil whispered to Patchouli.

'You run along... Mr Rockstar. Go on, do one,' said Wantha. 'Shouldn't you be going to pick up my sista?'

'Oh, Small Paul's giving her a lift,' Patchouli answered for Gil.

'Small Paul all the way from Todmorden, is it?'

'Yes, they'll probably arrive before we do with all this messing about.'

Wantha snapped shut a mini makeup compact mirror. 'Ready now innit,' Wantha led the way outside. This was the best possible version of herself. Shapely in Spanx, new hairdo (courtesy of Dimoda Hair Design). A new dress (courtesy of internet shopping). Pouted lips (courtesy of her own resting bitch face). She wore no perfume, relying on her own natural scent. Gil Von Black unlocked his car's doors, therefore inviting the two women in. And if you thought Matteo Dubois' car was well fancy, you should see this one. Wantha hid her admiration and sparked up a cigarette in the back. Gil Von Black forced his foot on the brake pedal, looking behind him at Wantha without moving his sunglasses. Wantha put the cigarette out in her hand... And there, the line was set.

Back at Number One Curmudgeon Avenue, Ricky Ricketts let himself in via the back door, followed by his heavily pregnant girlfriend, Gemma Hampsons. 'Alright, Mum,' he said.

'Oh! Oh, you gave me a shock!' Edith instinctively darted behind the door to the under the stairs cupboard, but the large plastic laundry basket she had left there earlier pushed her out of the way. Edith could not help noticing how Gemma looked at her, Edith, with her shiny face and her floral nightdress. Ricky had his head in the fridge. Harold had only just finished in the bathroom and was now bounding down the staircase.

'Ahh hello, hello!' he shook Gemma's hands with both his hands, which were still slightly damp from his bathroom adventure. Gemma smiled a smile that did not reach her eyes. 'So, will you be, you know, taking notes?'

'Pardon?' Gemma said.

'You know, that's what you journalists do, isn't it?'

'Don't be soft, Harold,' said Ricky, returning with the first of many cans of lager.

'I still haven't forgotten about that black pudding story incident,' Harold said in a half-joking, half-serious voice.

'Oh, stop with that nonsense, Harold. Anyway, you forgot the olives when you went shopping. Everyone has olives at Tiffin,' Edith said. She had now put on a voice that sounded like Edna. 'Please go to Mrs Ali's and see if she has any this instant.'

'Ohh, this instant!' Harold and Ricky laughed.

'Sit down, love, look, I just need to go and get ready, I've not had the chance to have… to get changed.'

'You look fine, Mum, you always wear that kind of dress,' said Ricky.

'Oh, this is my nightie!' Edith let out a deafening shrieking laugh and then set off to run upstairs. When she reached the sixth step, she slipped and came tumbling down the staircase, landing at the vestibule door with her nightdress around her waist.

'You OK, Mum?' Ricky shouted.

'Oh, yes, nothing to worry about!' said Edith,

hastily getting up off the floor and pulling her nightdress half down, half-tucked into her knickers.

'Maybe we should go and check?' said Gemma.

'No, you're pregnant. Sit down,' said Ricky.

Edith made another attempt at climbing the stairs, but there was a knock at the front door. Not Harold again, she rolled her eyes. 'Don't worry, I'll get it!' Edith shouted with half-sarcasm. She entered the vestibule, the frosted glass pane telling the story of not one, not two, but three people. *Who the bloody hell is this now? And I'm still in my nightdress!* She opened the door and was met by a greeting that she had sorely missed over the past few months.

'Ediff!' Toonan said with wide, outstretched arms.

'Toonan, oh!' Edith accepted the embrace from her little Whitefield friend while eying up the two strangers over Toonan's shoulder. 'What are you doing here?'

'Oh shit, Ediff, don't tell me we've got the wrong day? Typical Mum forgetting everything... She said she was coming round today, not some other day!'

'No, she is coming round today. I just didn't realise that erm that, never mind Toonan.'

'Sorry, Ediff, this is Francesca. We met in a lift the other day. You don't mind one more, do you?'

'No, I suppose…' Edith didn't even know Patchouli had invited Toonan and was now not minding three more.

'Hang on; let me do this properly…' Toonan stood back from Small Paul (what are you going to do? Carry him over the threshold?) 'This, Ediff, is Small Paul. Small Paul, this is Ediff, the one I was telling you about,' Toonan threw her left arm around Edith's shoulders as though she was some long lost aunt.

'Hello, Small Paul, hello Francesca,' Edith held out her hand to shake theirs.

'It's just Paul, really.'

'Sorry, hello, Just Paul. And oh did Toonan say you met in a lift?' said Edith, addressing Francesca.

'Yeah, we did,' Toonan answered for Francesca, aww I've got so much to tell you, Ediff, I've started a new job, and I was at The Met Theatre, and Francesca was in the lift, and then the lift stopped.'

'And that's where I came in, I rescued them,' said Small Paul.

'No, that's not the best of it. Francesca is…'

'Well, we're not sure; we need to find out if we're talking about the same man,' said Francesca.

'Francesca is… aww, wait until Wantha gets

here, she knows about this. Francesca is Matteo Dubois' ex-wife!' Toonan said, all wide-eyed.

'Well, we weren't actually married. Are you sure it's Matteo Dubois that you have living next door?'

'Yeah, that's 'im,' said Ricky sauntering down the hallway to see what all the fuss was about.

'Is Wantha coming ASWELL?' said Edith, mentally adding up the emergency chairs in her head.

'What!' said Ricky. 'Wantha's coming?'

'Yessss…' Yet another visitor arrived. 'Yes, she is Ricky Ricketts. Wantha Rose has just entered the building.' Wantha (still speaking about herself in the third person) pushed Toonan and Small Paul out of the way and grabbed hold of Edith in a bear hug. 'Ediff, I've missed you, hun…' Wantha said, all the while giving Ricky Ricketts the death stare.

'Where's your mother?' muffled Edith. *And why did you walk straight past me in Marks and Spencer?* She thought.

'Oh, they're just finding a parking space innit,' said Wantha, who was yet to let go of her long lost Edith.

'Well, you'd better all come through,' Edith struggled to free herself and led the way back down the hall, baring one buttock cheek as her nightdress was still tucked into her knickers. The party met Harold halfway, who had Mrs Ali in tow.

'Hello darling, I've had to shut the shop up. You should have given me fair warning you were having a get-together, Edith. Oh, hello, Wantha, I haven't seen you for ages (she winked) and hello Toonan. And Patchouli, darling!' Mrs Ali scanned the other guests that she had either not met yet, or had only previously gossiped about.

'Well, we can't all stand here in the hallway,' said Harold.

Gil Von Black let out a sigh of relief. His arms were killing him after cradling what appeared to be twelve magnums of Prosecco for longer than was reasonably necessary.

'Let's go in the front room,' Edith opened the door, where she saw Ricky and Gemma engaging in some heavy petting. 'Oh, maybe not, let's go in the backroom.' Too late, Edith, everyone had started piling into the front room. Ricky's face was as red as a beetroot. Gemma stood up for two reasons, one to show off her heavy gestation, the other to meet Wantha eye-to-eye.

'Hello, Wantha,' Gemma said, stroking her middle with smug satisfaction.

'Innit,' Wantha clicked, making no sense at all.

CHAPTER 26: CAUSE FOR CONCERN ON TWO COUNTS.

Over the following few days at Chateau le Grincheaux, life continued in much the same vein. Wine bottles were drained. French cuisine (cooked by a Scot) was consumed, and Genevieve continued with her claptrap. On the day the builders returned to complete further works to the roof and chimneys, Genevieve had been spotted half-dressed in the bedroom window blowing kisses at the males. '*French sense of humour,*' she had explained. Mr and Mrs Bove had engaged in what was now their nightly visit to the spy hole, but they were none the wiser about their houseguests. Today, it was Genevieve's turn to arrive downstairs first and without Edna.

'Bonjour!' she sang as she skipped to the table

and helped herself to coffee and croissants. 'What a beautiful day it is today.'

'Somebody slept well,' said Jackson, turning his newspaper over.

'Like a baby,' said Genevieve, flipping her sunglasses down over her eyes.

'Erm, where's Edna?' said Diane, noticing the time. It was no longer breakfast time, not really.

'She is still asleep,' Genevieve pulled her lips down briefly and shrugged while heaping sugar into her cup. Diane and Jackson looked at one another. Edna was usually down before Genevieve. On the rare occasion that Genevieve arrived first, she had beaten Edna to the shower. The breakfast table's tension was almost unbearable and went on for quite some time. Genevieve was just about to announce that she would head outside to her usual sun lounger spot but then noticed the weather becoming overcast outside. She sat down again. The silence was broken by someone thundering and slipping down the wooden staircase.

'Edna?' Diane said, noting that Genevieve appeared unconcerned that her lover had almost taken a tumble.

'Oh, sorry about that, I must've slipped!' This morning, it was Edna's turn for the oversized sunglasses. She made it to the breakfast table, putting her handbag next to her plate. Edna broke wind loudly as she sat (which interrupted Diane asking her if she could get her a fresh pot of coffee). 'Oh, excuse me! Oh, please forgive me!'

Genevieve pursed her lips in disgust. It was unclear if this was because of Edna's fart or Diane's keenness to make Edna a fresh pot of coffee. Diane had ignored Genevieve's need for fresh coffee only half an hour earlier.

'Oh, that would be lovely, thank you,' said Edna. She removed her sunglasses to reveal a pair of the baggiest eyes that Mr and Mrs Bove had ever seen around their breakfast table.

'Oh!' said Diane.

'I know!' said Edna. 'I slept like a lead weight last night. Oh, I need this coffee, I've brushed my teeth, but my mouth feels awful.'

'Keep your sunglasses on, mon amie,' said Genevieve. She was itching to go outside for a cigarette, but it was clearly going to rain. Further pleasantries were exchanged, and Edna started rummaging around in her handbag. 'I'm looking for my vitamins,' she was saying.

'Oh, well, you're welcome to have some of my cod liver oil capsules, my mother swore by those until she died at age ninety-two,' said Diane, passing the tub over to Edna. But Edna's hand had fallen on something familiar, which she pulled out of her handbag and removed her sunglasses so that she could examine it.

'Oh, oh how silly of me! I must've got my sleeping tablets mixed up with my vitamins!' Edna looked over the top of her sunglasses. 'They're occasional sleeping tablets, you understand. I only use them for travel... I must've put my occasional sleeping tablets next to my bed and my night-time vitamins in my handbag. How odd,' Edna replaced her sunglasses. Mr and Mrs Bove looked at one another with married couple knowing looks. Genevieve took in the entire scene of glances and unspoken assumptions.

'Well, we are going for a walk today to make the most of the French autumn,' Genevieve announced. 'You are welcome to join us.'

Feeling invited but not welcome, Diane and Jackson stumbled over their words to make excuses about gardening and getting the chateau ready for the next time the builders would be here.

'Very well,' said Genevieve, wrapping a pashmina around her shoulders. Edna was still engrossed in her own vitamin mystery. 'Come on, Edna, stop fussing over your potions. I take this to keep me young, I take this to wake me up, I take this occasionally. Night-time vitamins? Pah, we all know you mean laxatives!' Genevieve mimicked Edna, which did her no favours regarding the observations and assumptions that Mr and Mrs Bove were making.

'Ah, very well, let's go on our walk, Genevieve.' Edna gathered her pile of paraphernalia and scooped it back into her handbag.

As the two women commenced their activity in their matching flat shoes, pashminas and sunglasses, Diane and Jackson took up their positions in the upstairs room with the best window.

'I knew these binoculars would come in handy one day,' said Diane. Mr and Mrs Bove watched Edna and Genevieve walking away from the chateau for quite some time. They walked at the side of the road, zig-zagging through fields and then commenced the hill towards the forest.

'Give me a look!' said Jackson, focussing in on the pair. 'Oh, for goodness sakes, they're going off-road! They're going into the forest!' Diane snatched the binoculars from her husband's face.

'I can't see them!'

'Here, let me have another look. Oh my God, I can't see them either now. I'll have to go in after them!' Jackson said. He was right; in that brief moment when the Boves exchanged binoculars, Edna and Genevieve had disappeared into the trees.

'You can't go in after them! Not straight away… They'll know we've been spying on them!' Diane clutched the binoculars close to her like a naughty child clutching a stolen bag of sweets.

'I'll go,' said Jackson, hearing the doorbell. 'You keep looking, Diane.' She did just that, concentrating on the scene in the woods, she heard lots of hearty laughter coming from downstairs.

'What were you laughing at?' Diane said when Jackson returned.

'French sense of humour, my arse, I've just shown the builders that wanted poster of Genevieve, and they thought it was hilarious!'

.....

'Give me your hand; it's not too steep once you get up here,' said Edna to Genevieve. That's right, Edna was leading the way. 'Oh look, look up there ahead, a clearing in the forest!' Edna said.

'Yes, but we must be careful; who do you think made this clearing?' said Genevieve. Edna's mind flickered over the possible scenarios. Who *had* made the clearing? Youths and hoodlums? Not in this part of France, surely. Farmers? Why would they? Campers? No, surely the tent dwellers of France would more than likely stay in one of the many boutique custom-made campsites complete with facilities.

'The clearing? Well, it obviously occurs naturally, and look, there is a fallen tree trunk we can sit on,' said Edna.

'That tree trunk has not fallen of its own accord,' said Genevieve. 'A pack of French boars has felled it.'

'Don't be ridiculous. Little pigs can't knock a tree over, even a family of them.' Edna placed two squares of towel onto the tree trunk and sat down. 'It was most likely struck by lightning, or maybe it just fell down of old age. Trees don't last forever, you know!' Edna sounded as though she knew what she was talking about and patted the seat beside her for Genevieve to sit on. But Genevieve had now lit a cigarette and was pacing up and down the clearing with her arms folded. It was a bit on the dark side in there, with only shards of light streaming through the remaining trees, yet both women still had their sunglasses in situ.

'Boars are not leetle pigs,' Genevieve Frenched it up. 'They are wild animals… wild!' she used her hands to make a clawing expression. 'They will come here, and they will head butt us. That is how they got rid of that tree.'

Edna was now making herself at home. Having set up her outdoor easel, she prepared the area to do some light sketching. Artist's A5 sized sketchbook, pencils of all different grades, soft and hard. Even some charcoal and artist's sponges. Edna started measuring up her chosen area with her thumb and forefinger. Giving the impression of measuring perspective and that she knew what she was doing. Genevieve was still pacing and looking uneasy.

'You know...' said Edna in between impressions. 'If those little piggies are around here, they will most likely hear you and all your twig snapping that is going on beneath your feet!' said Edna.

'Ohhh,' Genevieve made a French-sounding sigh and sat down next to Edna.

'They are nocturnal animals I believe, so I shouldn't worry too much,' said Edna, continuing with her illusion of being a professional painter.

'Why don't we carry on walking? We are meant to be going for a walk, not going for an art lesson!' huffed Genevieve. 'Anyway, it looks as if it is almost dark now; the boars or the leetle piggies will be thinking it is waking up time!'

'It was your idea to come out, Genevieve. I just don't see the point of coming out *just* for a walk. I would like to do something creative when I get to my destination before turning back home,' Edna looked over at her companion, who was biting her fingernails. 'Are you bored?'

'Non, I am not bored.'

'Why don't you play *Candy Crush*.'

'Because I do not 'ave my phone.'

'Oh dear,' said Edna as though she was speaking to a child. 'Do you want to read something on my Kindle?'

Genevieve huffed and fumbled around in Edna's bag finding her Kindle. She then had to find a short but entertaining book to read in a comfortable position.

'You should be able to find some French books, although the ones I have downloaded already are in English,' Edna said, now making long marks on her paper.

Genevieve raised an eyebrow; she had not even considered this. 'I can understand English.' (Yes, you can, Genevieve.) After various different positions, including sitting astride the tree trunk with her back resting against Edna, Genevieve decided it was no good. She was unable to find a comfortable place. She let out a huge French sigh and made several tutting sounds. She stood up.

'Edna, it is time we were getting back,' Genevieve said.

'Nonsense! We have only just sat down!' said Edna.

'Hufffff!' said Genevieve.

As you can well imagine, this little episode of bickering went on for longer than was reasonably necessary. Edna needed to rest a while before walking back to the chateau, even if it was downhill.

Back at the chateau, Mr and Mrs Bove were

on tenterhooks waiting for the return of their houseguests, their own search for them a couple of hours earlier being fruitless. The sky had gone from romantically overcast to downright filthy, it looked as though it was about to rain, and just as that same rain started, the front door opened.

'Oh, thank goodness!' said Diane. The two of them rushed downstairs, welcoming the sorry sight of an angered Genevieve Dubois at their front door.

'Bonjour,' she said, rather tersely.

'Oh, hello, we were getting worried about you... two.'

'Why?' Genevieve barked.

'Well, you know,' said Diane.

'It's going to start raining, and where IS Edna?' said Jackson.

'Ah! I killed her and buried her in the forest...' said Genevieve matter of factly.

'WHAT!' Mr and Mrs Bove exclaimed in horror at Genevieve, who started uncontrollably laughing.

'Ha! That is what you are thinking, isn't it?' Genevieve could hardly get her words out for laughing. 'See, ahh, my friends, French sense of humour, I told you is different from the British!' Genevieve tried to embrace the Boves in her friendship. 'Edna is, she is probably following me, and how do you British people explain it? We had a slight disagreement!' Genevieve gestured small with her forefinger and thumb. 'Tiny... Edna wanted to stay to carry on scribbling on her pad... And I was bored. I wanted to come back here, that is all.' Genevieve made her way inside, helped herself to a tumbler of whisky and ice and flopped onto the couch. Diane rushed outside to (hopefully) see Edna coming down the path towards her, but she was not there, and the rain was starting to feel like it was going to be a massive storm.

'She was not following you, Genevieve!'

'Don't worry, she will get here eventually. She's stubborn.' Genevieve drained her glass and poured herself another. Jackson snatched out of her hand, surprising himself at his own vigour.

'Sorry,' he stood back, only there have been reports of wild boars in those woods. I think we should go in after her; you'll have to show us where she was.'

'French sense of humour, my arse!' Diane said under her breath.

CHAPTER 27: THERE IS NO SMOKING ALLOWED IN THE PORSCHE.

'So how far along are you?' Patchouli eyed up Gemma Hampsons' big belly.

'Oh, hahaha, oh, I can't remember what the midwife said, Mrs... erm.'

'Rose,' Patchouli snapped. Wantha sucked in her cheeks and gave Ricky Ricketts the death stare with her tear denying filled eyes. Toonan started counting on her fingers.

'Oh hahaha,' Gemma embraced her own stomach on either side of her bulge. 'What is that you're doing?'

Patchouli had removed one of her fake crystal-drop earrings and dangled it, circling Gemma's baby bump. 'It's a crystal,' said Patchouli.

'Oh, like a healing crystal to make baby calm?' said Gemma.

'No,' said Patchouli. 'It's to see how far gone you are,' Patchouli then ceased the circling motion, replaced her earring and turned to whisper to Mrs Ali. 'Well, she's a crafty one, isn't she?'

'Awkward!' whispered Toonan to Francesca and Small Paul, neither of whom had a clue about the dynamics going on here.

'Tiffin is served in the drawing-room!' announced Harold.

'D'ya mean Mum's back room?' said Ricky.

'Yes,' nodded Harold. They all made their way (Harold first) into the back room, where an excited Edith met everyone with fussy descriptions of 'finger food'. Harold kept interrupting with mentions of his signature dish, 'Radcliffe hors d'oeuvres'. There were so many bodies present that the get together formed the socialising structure of '*mingling*', as you might expect at a wedding reception, or perhaps, a funeral. Gil Von Black was even taller than Harold, where Harold was a lanky streak of piss; Gil was a fine figure of a man.

'What line of work are you in, Gil?' Harold said. (If I had eyes, I would have rolled them at this point, as this line of questioning usually means, 'how much money have you got?')

'Oh, well, I was...' Gil decided against revealing his part in rock history. 'Nowadays, I am a property developer around here.'

'Around Curmudgeon Avenue?' said Harold, with a hint of disdain.

'Around Whitefield and Prestwich, popular with commuters,' said Gil. All the while, Patchouli was glancing from one tall man to the other.

'He drives a Porsche, Harold,' said Patchouli nodding at Gil.

'Yesss, and there's no smoking allowed in it, is it...' said Wantha, addressing Harold but giving Gemma Hampsons the evil eye.

'Well, that's my car, my love... I do have plans, though, for P and myself,' Gil Von Black put his arm around Patchouli.

'P? Who the fuck's P?' said Wantha.

'Your mother, dear, and I hope she will join me when I go to live in the States for six months,' said Gil. Wantha clicked her tongue in his face and turned away from them.

'Oh, the States is it?' said Harold.

'Innit!' Wantha flicked her head back.

'Yeah,' said Gil. Patchouli grinned and nodded, because let's face it, there is nowhere for this conversation to go.

Mrs Ali gave Gemma Hampsons a taste of her own investigative journalism medicine. 'So, thirty weeks? That would mean that this baby was conceived six, almost seven months ago. Hmm, I must try and think back to what was happening six, almost seven months ago.'

'You didn't get Gemma pregnant, Mrs Ali!' Ricky laughed.

'I know, Ricky, you got Gemma pregnant,' Mrs Ali said. Wantha was listening to this exchange, peeping over the top of Mrs Ali's shoulder...

'So I just knew that these two were going to make a happy couple when I saw the way that Toonan looked at Small Paul through the crack in the broken lift,' Francesca looked at her new friends with adoration.

'Oh, that's lovely, sweetheart,' said Edith. 'But what about you, Francesca?'

'Oh, I'm having some 'me' time at the moment. I went through a very difficult breakup.'

'Yeah, so did I innit,' said Wantha, destroying yet another conversation and glass of Prosecco while swinging round to the pregnant couple to give them a filthy look.

'Aww, she still lets him see the dog on face time. I think it's well cute... Small Paul,' Toonan said, addressing her new boyfriend. 'If we ever get a dog and then split up, I want you to know, I will let you see the dog on face time too.'

Francesca sighed.

'That's why I wanted to bring Francesca around here,' Toonan continued.

'Oh no, please, I don't want to make a fuss,' said Francesca. Everyone was now listening to this little conversation.

'You're not making a fuss, don't be soft. At least find out if your Matteo Dubois is the same as our Matteo Dubois.'

'Do you mean your sex pest?' said Wantha, now finishing off the Radcliffe hors d'oeuvres.

'Shh!' said Toonan.

'What?' laughed Francesca.

'I thought he was a fraud investigator,' said Mrs Ali, which was very cheeky of her because she knew exactly what had happened.

'No, he's my boss. He's opening up a shop in the next few months,' Ricky Ricketts said. Mrs Ali plucked up her ears. 'But I'm sworn to secrecy.'

'Yes, we can't afford for Richard to lose his job in our situation,' Gemma Hampsons rubbed that oversized belly of hers (it's even starting to get on my nerves now). Naturally, Toonan and Wantha gave Gemma a look that almost killed her and her innocent child. *'Richard?'* Wantha mouthed to Toonan.

'Why don't we invite him around? Might as well; everyone else is here,' said Harold. He went to open the back door, and Matteo Dubois was right there, peeping over the wall in the back yard.

CHAPTER 28: AS CONCERN GROWS FOR EDNA, GENEVIEVE HATCHES A PLAN.

Genevieve and Mr and Mrs Bove returned to Chateau le Grincheaux after a lengthy search of the forest. It was bizarre; Genevieve just could not find the clearing that she and Edna had visited earlier in the day. She genuinely was not doing it on purpose. She had no reason not to find Edna, it was throwing it down with rain now, and Genevieve just wanted to return home.

'Maybe she has found shelter elsewhere,' said Jackson... wistfully.

'Oh, I hope so, the weather is terrible tonight. Did Edna have a jacket with her?' said Diane.

'I can't remember,' Genevieve waved the questions away. Diane and Jackson looked at one another.

'Maybe we should report her missing to the gendarmerie?' said Jackson.

'She will be back; she's not the outdoorsy type,' said Genevieve. Mr and Mrs Bove debated the official reporting of Edna's disappearance privately. Genevieve tried to ring her mobile, but it went straight to voicemail. After being outside in the cold and rain, she started to sniff and coughed a little.

'Oh no, don't say you are feeling under the weather now,' said Diane.

'Oh, I'm fine...' But then it crossed Genevieve's mind that she needed to get out of the pending Paris trip. 'Actually, I think you are right. I think I'm coming down with something again,' Genevieve gently coughed into her scarf. 'I'd better get to bed; Edna will probably come home when she has finished sulking...'

Diane and Jackson watched Genevieve walk up the stairs to her bedroom. 'Well, this is a funny how do you do? How on earth can a woman go missing in a forest?'

'I know, and in this weather too.'

'It's the boars I'm worried about.'

Mr and Mrs Bove waited up for Edna for quite some time, falling asleep in one another's arms on the wicker couch. 'What time is it, Husband?' said Diane.

'I think it's about two in the morning,' said Jackson. Unlike their indifferent houseguest, the concerned couple decided they might as well retire to bed for a couple of hours and then resume the search when it became light. 'We'll leave the conservatory doors open for her, just in case,' whispered Diane.

Morning light arrived all too quickly, as so often it does in France. Diane jumped out of bed and opened her bedroom blinds. 'Oh, at least the rain has stopped.' Her first thoughts were about Edna. Could she really have been missing overnight, all night? She put on her dressing gown and slippers, and Jackson was ahead of her, already making his way downstairs. Genevieve was nowhere to be seen, despite her missing lover.

'You don't think?' Diane said to Jackson as they passed their bedroom door. 'No, we would've heard them last night; you're a very light sleeper.'

'Do you think we should have a quick look through the spy hole before knocking on their door?'

'No, let's go downstairs first,' Jackson said. Just then, there was a very loud coughing sound coming from Genevieve's bedroom. Diane and Jackson looked at one another with wide eyes, and a few moments later, Genevieve opened the door, squinting at her visitors.

'Bonjour?' she said.

'Morning, Genevieve,' Diane whispered. 'We're just about to go downstairs.'

'Yes, we weren't spying on you… why are you whispering, Diane?' said Jackson.

The three early birds crept downstairs, where they were met, right there, in the conservatory with the sight they had all been waiting for. Edna, looking bedraggled, was asleep on the wicker couch (which both Diane and Jackson were mentally preparing to replace following their current house guests' stay).

'Edna!' Genevieve rushed to her side. Edna said nothing, her voice, along with her senses, lost in her bedraggled appearance.

'Put the kettle on, Husband,' said Diane. 'You need a hot cup of coffee to warm you up, och, you've been out there all night and, oh, your clothes are ripped! What has happened to you?'

Edna did not and could not answer. Genevieve put her arm around her shoulder, but discovering that Edna was wet through and smelt of compost, she removed herself. As Jackson arrived with the tray of coffee, having set the fire going, he noticed something screwed up in Edna's claw-like hand. Genevieve removed it. Edna was still silent, and when the paper unravelled, there was a gasp. Genevieve put her hand over her mouth. She had been correct all along; scribbled on to the paper was one of Edna's pencil and charcoal drawings. It was an angry image, unmistakably of a wild boar. Wild in the eyes and wild in the claw. Reaching forwards for its prey, the woman who was hurriedly trying to capture its image, before it had launched itself at her. Edna silently made her way upstairs. Barefoot and leaving a dirty rain trail behind her with her tattered outfit. Which had been ripped away by wild boars teeth before he forced himself on her.

.....

'I must've been knocked unconscious, the animal pushed me, I fell, hitting my head on that tree trunk,' Edna spoke in a quiet voice. There was not a flared nostril in sight. Genevieve helped Edna into the bath and immediately started thinking of herself... she started coughing and spluttering.

CHAPTER 29: SHE PRONOUNCED HIS NAME 'MATCHEUR'

'Matcheur! It is you!' Francesca gasped and clutched her hands around her face. Matteo looked into Francesca's eyes. Curmudgeon Avenue's gawping residents surrounded the scene and almost made him lose it.

'What are you doing here?' he said.

'I met Toonan in a lift in the theatre I am working on at the moment. She happened to mention that she knew of a man who fitted your description recently moved next door to her friends. I can't believe it's you. I thought you were going to live in France!' said Francesca (not another one?)

'Yes, it's me, I'm trying Francesca, I'm trying to make a life for us, a permanent life. Next door!' Matteo said. He had Francesca at the word *'per-*

manent'. After all, It had been his lack of commitment that had made her end it in the first place, even though they had a dog together. Small Paul put his arm around Toonan in smug satisfaction of devoted coupled-ness.

'But why didn't you tell me?' Francesca said.

'I wanted to try and make a success out of the shop...'

'The SEX shop!' Mrs Ali interrupted with a pointed finger.

'What? No, it's not a sex shop. I'm going to open a delicatessen.' Matteo answered Mrs Ali, the secret fun he had had at her expense was now over. 'I wanted to make a success of it before asking you to come back to me. Asking you... (Matteo could not believe he was going to say this in front of these nincompoops.) Asking you to marry me,' Matteo announced. Francesca and all the other women gasped with romance.

'Yes, Matcheur, yes! Shelley and I have missed you too much!' said Francesca.

'Oh, this was only meant to be Tiffin!' said Edith, wiping a tear from her eye.

'What about your mother though, Matcheur?' said Francesca.

'OMG wait, wait! I forgot to tell you, wait till you see this photo Wantha saw on Instagram!' Toonan released herself from Small Paul's embrace and went into the front room to retrieve her sister and rescue Ricky Ricketts at the same time. Everyone went into the back room.

'Matt!' Ricky said, shaking his boss's hand. 'Can't get enough of me, is it? You know it's Saturday, don't you?'

'I do; Harold just invited me round because Francesca is here.'

'Shut it, Ricky Ricketts, look at this photo of Genevieve that Edna sent me on Instagram the other day. Look at it!' said Wantha holding her mobile phone in the palm of her hand as though it was the Holy Grail.

'Oh, no, I don't think that is your mother. She was never blonde, was she?' said Francesca.

'That's Joanna Lumley!' said Small Paul, looking over Wantha's shoulder.

'Oh yes, that does look like Joanna Lumley! Why did Edna send you a photo of Joanna Lumley?' said Edith.

'That's what we thought, Ediff at first, but then we tried to remember our Castlebrook High School French.'

'Toonan was better at French than Wantha was,' interjected Patchouli.

'It says this woman, who is looking like your mum, sorry Matteo, is wanted by French police in connection with more than one murder!' said

Wantha. 'And you,' she pointed at Gemma. 'Can put your investigative journalism away. Don't be tight on Matteo Dubois. He is my sista's mate's boyfriend!'

'Yes, and he is *my* boyfriend's boss!' said Gemma. Wantha clicked her tongue.

'Oh, hang on, oh let me have another look, will you!' Edith was close to tears. 'This can only mean one thing! Edna has sent this message to Wantha because she needs rescuing!'

'Don't be silly, Edith,' said Harold, never keen to come to the rescue of his sister-in-law. 'She would've just telephoned if she needed rescuing.'

'Not if she's being held hostage,' said Gil Von Black, who was a big fan of all the American action movies, where folk are often held hostage.

'Well, what do you think, love?' Edith said to Matteo. It occurred to him that his welcome to Curmudgeon Avenue so far had been somewhat unwelcoming thanks to Harold and Edith. And as for Mrs Ali, secretly trying to thwart his business plans, pah! He really was in the mood for revenge against these fuddy duddy's. But fortunately for Curmudgeon Avenue, Francesca brought out the lovely side in him.

'I think my mother loves Edna very much, and I think this is a case of mistaken identity. This photo is obviously Joanna Lumley. I can't imagine why the French police would suspect her of murder. Or why she would hold Edna hostage, or why Edna would send you this post on Instagram,' said Matteo.

'Well, she didn't send it to ME. She just posted it… Don't you know how it works?' said Wantha.

'Edna is not being held hostage by my mother,' Matteo sighed.

'Well, look at what she has posted most recently, hmm.' Wantha scrolled her phone screen and showed everyone Edna's latest photo. It was the sketch of the wild boar that she had hurriedly scribbled moments before she was assaulted. 'See, she is being held hostage by an angry-looking pig, and she has only got paper and the phone to keep herself safe!' Wantha folded her arms.

What was meant to be a bit of Tiffin has resulted in plans to move to the States, a marriage proposal, speculation about Gemma Hampsons pregnancy, and concerns about Edna being held hostage by a little pig.

CHAPTER 30: PARIS!

Edna made a miraculous recovery from her night in the woods. It still hurt her to sit down, but she managed to avoid talking about it.

However, Edna did have plenty to say about their forthcoming trip to Paris. She had booked Genevieve and herself two nights at L'hotel du Dotta. Edna booked the train, the most romantic way to travel across France. She had packed a small case for herself, perfect for two night's stay in Paris. She had even resorted to packing Genevieve's case for her after she appeared reluctant to do it for herself. Diane and Jackson were getting a little sick of hearing about this trip to Paris, as indeed was Genevieve.

'Two nights is hardly anything for a trip to Paris,' said Diane.

'Oh, it will be perfect, a perfect romantic mini-break. We do need a break, don't we, Genevieve?'

'Oui,' Genevieve answered without emotion.

Diane and Jackson looked at one another.

'Oh, I can't wait,' Edna smiled to herself and looked up towards the sky. 'Mr Bove, I wondered if I could trouble you to give Genevieve and myself a lift to the train station tomorrow morning. I'll pay you, I have tried to book a taxi, but they don't seem to have a taxi service around here, not in the way they do in Manchester.'

'No problem, and it's no bother, you don't have to pay me,' said Jackson.

'Oh, you're so kind, so very kind,' Edna sighed. Wow! This being nice business is really starting to suit Edna!

'Well, come on, Genevieve, we should go up to bed to get a good night's sleep before we go to Paris; we have a lot of walking ahead of us,' Edna patted Genevieve gently on the arm.

'Well, goodnight then,' said Diane, her non-verbals indicated it was reading time; this historical fiction novel won't read itself. Edna practically skipped upstairs, followed by an indifferent Genevieve.

'I've been to Paris many times, my love…' Genevieve said to Edna. 'Many times.'

Poor Edna, she had never been to Paris before; why was Genevieve not excited for her? For someone with such a snobbish attitude, Edna failed to see Genevieve's shortcomings. That's infatuation for you. I suppose. Edna slept soundly, and Genevieve did not... She thought she could hear some whisperings from behind the print of Madame du Pompadour in their bedroom. Again.

The following morning, the sky was... unfortunately, as dull as dishwater. Edna and Genevieve had lazily wasted away the days of summer, and now that the year was starting to show signs of ending, the air had become damp and dismal. Some would say that there is no point visiting France for a holiday, the weather is much the same as it is in Manchester. Edna disagreed; there is *every* point in visiting France, *escaping* to France and enjoying the romance of Paris. The Eiffel tower, the food, the Louvre, the patisseries, the Arc de Triomphe, the food. Edna had it all planned out; Genevieve and herself were to visit Paris, eat, and get a crick in both of their necks after looking up at the tall monuments that Paris boasts. Then they would eat some more food in their hotel, L'hotel du Dotta, not just any food, French cuisine, and most likely drink some wine, French wine. Ahhh.

'Wake up! Wake up, Genevieve!' Edna said with a loud voice. 'We're going to Paris today!'

Genevieve put her pillow over her head, thus indicating she was not in the mood for Paris or Edna.

'Very well, I will have a shower first!' said Edna, who had already carefully selected her outfit for today. What she considered a 'dressy' turtleneck, dark coloured slacks and, of course, flat shoes for all that walking around art galleries once they arrived there. Edna was ready in no time and returned from the bathroom, arms outstretched. 'Genevieve! Genevieve, you really should be getting up and ready now!' she said. Genevieve clumsily dragged herself out of bed, taking her bedsheet with her to the bathroom.

'Merde,' she said.

'I hope that shower puts you in a better mood!' Edna teased. As a special treat, Edna decided to carry Genevieve's mini-break travel case downstairs for her, along with her own.

'Oh, bonjour monsieur!' Edna greeted their chauffeur for the morning, Jackson.

'Morning, Edna. Diane's just through in the breakfast room, making your coffee. Where's Genevieve?' said Jackson.

'Oh, I had a shower first; she'll be down presently. Genevieve's just as excited as I am about our trip to Paris!' Edna lied and glanced nervously up the stairs.

'These your cases? I'll put them in the boot of the car for you,' Jackson took the mini-break travel cases from Edna.

'I cannot thank you enough for giving us a lift to the train station,' said Edna, making her way towards the coffee and croissants.

'Bonjour, Edna, help yourself to breakfast,' said Diane, which Edna obeyed immediately. 'Where's Genevieve?'

Edna was about to launch into repeating exactly what she had said to Jackson when a little voice echoed, ''ere I am.' It was Genevieve slouching into the corner chair with an unlit cigarette in her mouth. She too had carefully selected today's outfit. A slouchy, baggy jumper cascading off her left shoulder with nonchalance, an indifferent black beret encased her entire head of hair and her large sunglasses. Even though she was inside. 'I know, Diane, I am not going to smoke zis inside,' she said, eyeing her hostess with a rebuttal.

'Or in the car, if you don't mind, Genevieve,' said Diane. Edna shoved her lower lip into her top lip with a chastising little smile towards Genevieve. Smoking can be rude sometimes, but Genevieve did it with such style. She huffed her way outside, and with one arm folded around her middle, paced up and down until that solitary cigarette had been sucked to death. She flicked its butt into the pool, which fortunately Diane did not see.

'Would you like some breakfast, Genevieve?' said Edna as bright as a button, with the remains of her croissant crumbs littered across her dressy turtleneck.

'Non,' Genevieve swallowed her black coffee in one single gulp.

'Right, let's set off then!' Edna squealed (it is at times like this that you can tell she is Edith's sister).

But Genevieve slumped back down onto the big chair. 'Non,' she repeated. Edna turned on her heel to face her.

'What do you mean no?'

'I mean, non, I am not coming,' said Genevieve. It is difficult to tell if she is giving Edna the death stare right now with those huge sunglasses on. 'I am sorry, my love,' she fiddled with her cigarette box.'I am not feeling up to it. I am unwell.'

'What! You're lying!' Edna clutched her mouth with both hands. 'I mean, you were alright yesterday!'

'I know,' Genevieve pulled out her lower lip and mimed a little cough. Diane was getting a crick in her neck from observing the two women's exchanges.

'What's the hold-up? I'm all ready to drop you two off at the train station out here, cases and everything in the boot!' said Jackson, having got fed up of waiting.

'Genevieve says she's not going,' said Diane, as

Edna crumpled with disappointment.

'Well, if you're unwell, then I suppose we can stay here. It's just a shame we wouldn't be able to postpone,' said Edna.

'Oh,' Genevieve coughed. 'Don't let me stop you, Edna, I know 'ow much you were looking forward to the cuisine!'

'Well, you'll have to decide now really, time's a bit tight for the train,' said Jackson, tapping his wristwatch face. Genevieve turned away from Edna, which slightly irked Diane. Here was Edna arranging and no doubt paying for a romantic mini-break. Yet Genevieve couldn't even be bothered to go.

'Well, I'd go if I was you, Edna,' said Diane. 'There's lots of people who go on city breaks alone these days; you'll be fine.' Genevieve received one of Diane's exclusive dirty looks.

'Well, are you coming or not?' Jackson said.

'Yes! Yes, I think I will!' Edna's head was lifted into the *nose in the air* position it usually was.

'That's the spirit!' Jackson and Edna made their way outside. Diane put her hands on her hips, ready to chastise the smirking Genevieve. The car engine started, and Edna looked behind her at Chateau le Grincheaux.

'Hang on! Hang on, Jackson!' Edna could see Genevieve running towards the car with no apparent signs of illness.

'You 'ave my mini-break travel case in the boot of your car!' said Genevieve as she caught up. Edna's face fell at the realisation that Genevieve had not changed her mind; she was not coming but did not want to be without her case. The noise of the car boot opening and shutting broke Edna's heart a little bit more. As did the train door closing, the whistle blowing and every chug over the train tracks until Edna arrived in Paris. Edna thought she would feel better once she saw the beautiful city that she had so desperately wanted to see. But all she saw was fog, and you know what fog leads to? Confusion.

CHAPTER 31: WHO THE HELL IS KATHLEEN HENSHAW?

Even before Mr Bove had returned from the train station, Genevieve had discarded her beret and slouch jumper. Replaced her sunglasses and resumed her position on the sun lounger. It was no longer sunny, but Genevieve had to smoke somewhere. With every drag she took, she returned the filthy look of disdain that Diane threw her way. How could she do this to Edna? Diane could not bear the thought of Edna being alone in the most romantic city in the world. She imagined the waiters taking pity on her, discreetly altering the place settings from two to one.

'Don't be sorrowful, Miss Payne,' they might say.

'She'll be fine,' said Jackson, reading his wife's

thoughts. 'You said yourself lots of people go on mini-breaks to the city alone, at least she won't have to speak French there. Everyone speaks English in Paris.'

'I know, I was just trying to be nice, you know I really thought she had changed her mind when I saw her running out towards your car, but she just came back in with her case.'

'Don't... You should've seen poor Edna's face. All I could see in the rear-view mirror was nostrils; the poor woman was trying her best not to cry.' Jackson flapped his own nostrils in imitation with his fingers. 'Come on, leave madam Smoky McSmoke-Face out there in the mist. We're going out later, it's date night, don't forget. I do not want my wife's mood to be clouded by the nonsense of others.'

Meanwhile, in Paris, the vista had turned gloomy. Edna, having decided the best way to deal with her lonely situation, would be to have a fantastic time and put plenty of photographs on social media, illustrating just how much of a fabulous time she was having. The first thing she needed to do, she decided, would be to eat and drink. And then take photos of the food and drink. This is exactly what she did—two soups in a special dish, which was two bowls in one piece of crockery. Snap! That one went on Facebook. Three cheese soufflé, snap! Twitter. Honey roast comfit of duck with a large glass of red wine. Snap! Instagram. People looked over at Edna; things were too awkward to offer to take a portrait for her. Some of her fellow diners even thought her uncouth.

Next on the itinerary of Edna's most fabulous time ever in misty Paris was the Arc de Triomphe. After paying the bill and consulting her tourist guide map, she set out walking in her flat shoes to the famous monument in Paris's centre. She had been walking for quite some time, past several signposts to the memorial. In fact, before she decided she was lost and probably would not be able to see the Arc de Triomphe, not unless it was lit up like that thing over there. Oh! That must be the Eiffel Tower! Edna's eyes brimmed with tears as she made out, inside a cloud, Paris's most famous landmark lit up like Madame du Pompadour. Edna turned on her heel, wondering if tourists could still access the viewing platform.

The evening arrived at Chateau le Grincheaux, as so often it did. Genevieve had spent the day smoking and drinking with absolutely no sign of illness. It was Mr and Mrs Bove's monthly date night, and they were ready to make their way to the local bistro for good food and wine (which would not necessarily make its way to social media).

'Right, Genevieve, we're off out now,' said Jackson. Genevieve raised one eyebrow at the pair; it would not take long for her to get ready for a party at the bistro.

'Where are you going?' Genevieve asked, removing herself from the sun lounger and shoving her feet into her shoes.

'Oh, no you don't!' said Diane.

'Pardon?' Genevieve smirked.

'I'm sorry, Genevieve, tonight is date night for my husband and myself. If you wanted date night, you should have gone to Paris with Edna!' Diane folded her arms. Jackson shrugged at Genevieve, who watched Mr and Mrs Bove disappear down their path. She then selected and stole another one of Diane's boxes of chocolates from its new hiding place and skipped upstairs to bed.

'What a lying bitch!' said Diane. 'Did you see that look? She wanted us to invite her out with us! She's supposed to be ill!'

'Or at least pretending to be ill!' agreed Jackson.

Back in Paris, Edna Payne strode towards her chosen tourist attraction, The Eiffel Tower. Lit up like a Christmas tree, the top invisible in the mist, the bottom looking almost lonely. Well, Edna, you and the tower will make a fine pair tonight. Get yourself up there and make sure you take lots of photos for Instagram, some of the views would be nice, but we can only wish for that today. Poor Edna, she had been unlucky even on the Eiffel Tower. She stood on the railed platform shrouded in mist. At least a tourist took pity on her and offered to take her photograph. After a few clicks, there was Edna, trying her best to smile; standing next to a rail, next to a cloud of fog. Screw Genevieve, she thought. Screw her!

Shortly after Edna's endeavour with the most French and famous tourist attraction and back in Whitefield, near Manchester... Wantha had persuaded her sister Toonan, and her new boyfriend, Small Paul from Todmorden, to accompany her to the Frigate public house. Small Paul had little if nothing in common with Wantha, so the conversation was strained. It was only natural, then that Wantha should start looking at Instagram.

'Oh – My - God!' Wantha said, getting the majority of the pub's current punters' attention. 'Toonan! I think Edna definitely has been kidnapped this time! I'm gonna have to tell Ediff! I've no credit, though! Ring me a taxi, someone!' Wantha showed her sister and Small Paul photographs from Edna's Instagram. Hardly a social media expert, Edna had failed to add any captions to explain her posts' relevance. So Wantha naturally had to make things up as she went along.

'This is food. Food and wine,' Wantha pointed

to the screen with her magenta coloured gel-nailed-finger. 'I bet they force-fed her that as her last meal.'

Toonan burst out laughing at the thought of Edna being 'force-fed' anything.

'This one,' said Wantha, all serious. 'This one is the holding pen they are keeping her in. Look at those railings. Look at Edna's face. And *LOOK* at all that fog behind the railing. I bet that's how they're going to kill her.' Wantha said, all wide-eyed and serious. 'They are going to kill her with a smoke machine.'

Wantha, Toonan and Small Paul (still on the latter two's date) made their way to Curmudgeon Avenue. To break the news to Edith that her sister Edna was missing, presumed kidnapped in France.

It was a good job that Edna decided to ditch the social media posting for that day, because on the way back to L'hotel du Dotta, she saw YET ANOTHER wanted poster, this time, as Parisians hardly ever speak French, it was written in bold English;

WANTED: MADAME KATHLEEN HENSHAW. THE BLACK WIDOW OF ROCAMADOUR.

Wanted in connection with the deaths of three men in Paris and Dordogne.

Although it was quite an old poster, the face that stared out at Edna was unmistakably the face of Genevieve. Yes, she did look a bit like Joanna Lumley, but the brunette on the photo was most definitely Madame Genevieve Dubois. So who the hell was Kathleen Henshaw? A name that could not be more English if it tried. When Edna returned to her hotel room, there had been another unfortunate turn of events. Edna had brought Genevieve's case with her instead of her own... This was also Genevieve's fault because of all the messing about when Jackson was driving them to the train station. She unzipped it and hoped she could salvage and squeeze herself into some of Genevieve's garments. Edna tried but failed to pull Genevieve's pyjamas leg over her knee. Edna resigned herself she would have to rinse out her knickers like a Girl Guide and hoped they dried overnight. But what was this? Shoved into the front compartment of Genevieve's mini-break travel case was a FRENCH PHRASEBOOK!

Why on earth did Genevieve need a French phrasebook?

CHAPTER 32: SHE WASN'T LYING.

Poor Edna with her anticlimactic fog-laden visit to Paris. Screw Genevieve! She had thought with a belly full of French cuisine and wine. Screw her! Refusing to engage in a romantic mini-break, screw her!

The train journey back to Chateau le Grincheaux had been spent in a bizarre social media conversation with Wantha Rose, her disagreeable nephew's on/off girlfriend. This was the first time Edna realised that she was being *'followed'* by Wantha. They agreed, should Edna ever return to Whitefield, to a lesson in all things Twitter. Edna confirmed that she was alive and well and that her visit to Paris had been enjoyable, yet disappointingly misty. Edna learnt all about her nephew's indiscretions and that she was to become a great-aunt. Although unfortunately (or fortunately depending on your point of view), Wantha was not the mother of the forthcoming bundle of joy.

Edna was told that Wantha and Edith had been

cheating on Gemma Hampsons by secretly meeting up with each other. The pair missed their one-time mother-in-law/daughter-in-law bond. And, the new neighbour on the street was none other than Matteo Dubois, Genevieve's adopted son! Looking for his mother and wanting to live in the house they had lived in previously! Edna could not bear any more of this Genevieve talk and so politely signed off her private message chat with Wantha. 'L8tRs' was the reply Edna received.

Edna sat back in her train seat and sighed. She had tried her best to escape from Curmudgeon Avenue. Yet here she was, alone on a train private messaging Whitefield's very own princess. Edna shut her eyes, the last few minutes of that train journey giving her time to think through the facts that had been thrust upon her. (And I don't mean the soap opera status of her nephew's swimmers). It was the fact that Genevieve really was, or had, at some point, been known as Kathleen Henshaw, whoever *that* was. And she was wanted in connection with the deaths of three men all across France! Aside from the fact of Genevieve's deception, Edna flared her nostrils and raised her head in preparation for the realisation that Genevieve had been using her to escape France. Then when she had realised that her son, Matteo, followed her back to Whitefield. Genevieve had used Edna once again to escape from Curmudgeon Avenue (although why she wanted to hide from her son was anyone's guess). Now, all that Northumberland nonsense made sense. Genevieve had not really wanted to return to France at all because she was wanted by the police, so it seems. Now the beret and large sunglasses made sense. Now the different names made sense. Oh, what a tangled web we weave, when first we practice to deceive… GENEVIEVE!

Edna managed to employ a taxi to drive her back to Chateau le Grincheaux from the train station. The taxi driver had plenty to say about the goings-on at the chateau, but Edna could not understand his French. She paid the fare, and as the taxi crept up the path, Edna was stunned by the sight of police cars; the gendarmerie had arrived at the chateau! Edna failed to see the other official vehicles parked in the driveway. Screw Genevieve! She thought as she thanked the taxi driver and entered the front door holding the French phrasebook in her hand; this was her proof that Genevieve had been lying all that time. That the visiting police were correct! They had found her! The black widow of Rocamadour! Screw you, Genevieve. Edna is ready for you!

But when the front door of the chateau opened, Edna was met by a sight she was not expecting. Diane, noticing that Edna had arrived home, had rushed out, holding both her hands over Edna's hands (discarding the French phrasebook).

'Oh Edna, she wasn't lying. She *was* ill. I'm so sorry, Edna, you'd better come inside and sit down. I'm so sorry Edna, it's about Genevieve, we found her... She's... oh Edna... we found Genevieve dead in her bed, we've been trying to get hold of you.'

'Dead?!' said Edna, open-mouthed.

'Come on inside,' said Jackson, putting his arm around Edna. Diane was still holding her hands. A stretcher was wheeled out with a sheet fully covering the body of Genevieve Dubois (or whoever she was).

'Genevieve,' Edna cried, putting her hands over her face; she trembled all the way over to the stretcher and tried to peel back the sheet.

'Non-Madame!' the paramedic said to Edna.

'Edna, I've identified her, she... Don't look at her, not until the funeral people have seen to her,' said Jackson, holding Edna gently by the arm.

'Oh, but I think I found something out when I was in Paris,' Edna said, retrieving the French phrasebook. 'I feel so guilty.'

'Oh poor love, you've nothing to feel guilty about. You've had a terrible shock,' Diane said, leading Edna inside.

Diane helped Edna to settle into the comfortable sitting room; Edna would probably not want to stay in the bedroom tonight. Although Edna insisted she has a look, she had many questions; they all did. Genevieve was only complaining of a cough; surely you can't die from just a cough?

She had not died of just a cough, well, not really. After stealing Diane's box of chocolates, Genevieve had popped them in her mouth, one after the sneaky next one. That's the problem with hard centred confection. Popping them into your mouth without due caution can cause a terrible choking accident if one of them should go down the wrong hole. If only Genevieve had understood the French writing on the box, warning her of such a miscalculation…

Do you know what sound a person makes when choking? They make no sound at all… The solid round chocolate-covered Brazil nut lodged itself into Genevieve's windpipe. There were two entrances but only one exit. She had gripped her own throat with both her hands and watched the panic seize her own body in the mirror. This was everyone's worst fear… choking to death in silence. Especially for the likes of Genevieve, she was not a pretty crier. Tainted chocolate saliva had rolled down her chin. Logic had escaped her, and she could not ask for help because Diane would know that she had stolen yet another box of chocolates. Her final thought was to push the box under the bed before crashing to the floor with a giant thud, which Mr and Mrs Bove did not hear, despite the spy hole, on account of it being date night.

'And then we knew sometimes she had slept in late, and it had always been you, Edna up bright and early. But when she hadn't surfaced by one PM, we thought we'd better check,' Diane finished the explanation of the previous twenty-four hours.

'It wouldn't have made any difference if we'd have gone in earlier in the morning. She was already... dea... she had already passed,' Jackson tried to be sympathetic (with fear of litigation at the back of his mind). They had never had a death at their chateau before, and out of this pair of guests, they had not expected it to be Genevieve.

'Then we called the emergency services, and then you arrived home. I thought you were staying for two nights in Paris?' said Jackson.

'I was originally, but...' Edna chose her words carefully here, not wishing to admit her ideal trip to Paris had been a washout. She blinked for longer than was reasonably necessary. 'I think I knew something was up, I just knew,' Edna wiped away a tear as Diane herself started crying again.

'I was like that when my mother passed, wasn't I Jackson, I just knew,' Diane said, and Jackson nodded.

'The thing is, Edna, and only when you're ready...' Jackson said.

'Oh, not yet, Jackson,' Diane hit her husband quite forcefully with the tissue she had been using to dry her eyes. 'She's had a shock; we can deal with the formalities tomorrow,' she turned to Edna. 'Or at a later date.'

'Oh my goodness, of course, do you want me to leave? Under the circumstances.'

'Oh no, nothing like that, it's just the police came because they couldn't find any identification in Genevieve's handbag...'

CHAPTER 33: EDITH CHEATS ON GEMMA HAMPSONS BY MEETING UP WITH WANTHA ROSE.

After Wantha's midnight mercy dash to Curmudgeon Avenue and encountering Harold in his pyjamas, Wantha had accepted Edith's invitation to meet up at Summerseat Garden centre. Not just any old garden centre, Summerseat Garden Centre boasted the most famous cafe in the area, frequented mainly by people in Harold and Edith's demographic (except posher). It was also a full ten miles in the opposite direction of Manchester, away from Curmudgeon Avenue. Edith had picked Wantha up – incognito wearing a headscarf and a pair of spectacles with no lenses in.

'What about your mother?' said Edith.

'What about her?'

'Well, I thought you were her full-time carer?' Edith whispered.

'Mum's fine, she's with that Gil Von Black one at his house, and his kitchen is well fancy. She's quite safe; she can't work the hob there.' Wantha clicked her tongue against the roof of her mouth.

Edith drove the pair of them to their secret location in the purple Morris Marina. She had not driven for quite some time, now that Harold had taken over, and so it took them longer than was reasonably necessary to get there. They made their way through the knick-knacks and garden accessories before reaching the self-service cafe and a corner table out of view.

'Hello, Edith!' Pauline Foote (remember her?) loudly caught Edith's attention. (Honestly! You cannot go anywhere privately in North Manchester these days).

'Hello,' returned Edith without removing her disguise. 'Don't worry, I don't think she knows Gemma Hampsons,' whispered Edith to Wantha. She nervously positioned her navy blue handbag.

'Nice to see you, Edith. Wantha,' said Pauline Foote, who had marched over to their table with her decorative walking stick. 'I was meant to be meeting my granddaughter, you know, Georgina's daughter, but I don't think she's coming.' Pauline looked at both women, in turn, waiting for a response. Neither of them gave a fig about Pauline or her missing granddaughter. Pauline, picking up on this, went for it. 'I hear congratulations are in order, Edith. I hear you're going to be a grandmother, like me!'

Wantha gave Edith her *'I'll deal with this'* look. 'Yeeeah, Ediff will be able to get stood up in the chronic's cafe too, just like you, Paul-ine,' she clicked loudly in Pauline Foote's ear. Edith smiled nervously, and Pauline excused herself from the scene. She immediately started tagging Edith and Wantha on Facebook with their location...

'Oh, I have missed you, Wantha, you, your sister, and your mother.'

'Aww, I've missed you too, Ediff,' said Wantha (notice how she didn't mention Harold).

'I'm so sorry about what our Ricky did.'

Wantha hesitated; she wanted to offer up her usual retort, *'Who?'* but of course, they both knew exactly who Ricky Ricketts is and what he had done.

'I blame myself,' said Edith, shaking her head in

shame.

'No, it's not your fault Ediff, don't be soft. I blame that Gemma Hampsons one,' Wantha drank her cappuccino and left a moustache of milk froth on her upper lip.

'So you're not angry at Ricky, not just a little bit?' Edith spoke with a hint of hopefulness.

'No more than usual, Ediff, but that Gemma one! She always had her eye on my boy; she just managed to catch him.'

'Well, you're right, he is your... boy... that's what I wanted to talk to you about, after Tiffin the other day..'

'Tiffin?'

'After we all met up the other day, Mrs Ali was keen to have a chat with me; she'd had a private word with your mother and, well, we all figured it out,' Edith said, like a *Scooby-do* ending. 'Gemma Hampsons is HEAVILY pregnant.'

'Innit,' said Wantha.

'I mean, Wantha, she is almost close to bursting. She is more like nine months pregnant, which means that...'

'Nine months ago was when Ricky Ricketts was doing that four-week stretch for drunk and disorderly,' said Wantha, with her own hint of hopefulness.

'So he can't be that baby's father, God forgive me for saying that about the poor little mite!' Edith crossed herself, and she isn't even Catholic.

'It's well tricky, though because of dates and stuff, we can't be sure. If Ricky did get Gemma pregnant just before he got sent down, that would mean that your son,' Wantha folded her lips together and sucked in a load of air through her nose. 'That *your son* cheated on me.'

Edith gasped and put her hand over her shamefaced mouth. She had been hoping to happily solve things.

'While drunk and disorderly,' Wantha added in disgust.

'Oh, oh, I'm so sorry, Wantha. I was hoping to make things better, but I think I've made them worse.'

'Ah, no worries, Ediff, and anyway, I have some good news for you,' said Wantha.

'Yes?' said a hopeful Edith.

'The other day, I decided I'm going to let Ricky Ricketts love me again!' Wantha said with the triumph of a cat that has just domineered the family dog. Edith sank down into her chair with the disappointment of a cat that has discovered its cat biscuits have been stolen by the same family dog.

'But how? He's with Gemma now. They're living together in her semi-detached house on

Sunnybank Road,' said Edith.

'Ricky Ricketts cannot resist a bit of Wantha Rose; that's how Ediff!' Wantha sat back in her chair, triumphant once again. The situation now transformed into a game of cat and mouse.

Wantha instinctively started scrolling on her Smartphone. There was no further news of Edna, although the last that Wantha had heard was when Edna was on her way back to Chateau le Grincheaux, not kidnapped as previously thought. However, when observing Facebook, Wantha and Edith had something to thank Pauline Foote for. Pauline thought she was grassing Wantha and Edith up for meeting behind Gemma's back but had inadvertently hatched the two women's plans. *'Operation Wantha and Ricky'*. Wantha and Edith clinked their coffee cups together in celebration.

'Cheers,' they said which did not go down well in the garden centre cafe. Not in Summerseat Garden Centre cafe, anyway.

Meanwhile, in a semi-detached house on Sunnybank Road, Gemma Hampsons, her maternity leave in the second week, was having a quick look at social media.

'Ricky!' she hollered down her mobile phone. 'What the hell is your mother doing, cheating on me with Wantha Rose in Summerseat Garden

Centre?!'

CHAPTER 34: EDNA UNHINGED.

'What will happen about Genevieve?' were the first words out of Jackson's mouth when Mr and Mrs Bove woke the following day at the Chateau le Grincheaux.

'We should be more bothered about what's going to happen to poor Edna,' said Diane.

The pair ventured downstairs in unison, where they met the sorrowful picture of Edna in the breakfast room. Diane restrained Jackson with a gentle hand on her husband's midriff.

'Hello, Edna love, did you get any sleep?'

'No! Not really!' Edna said, all wide-eyed and even louder than usual. 'I made coffee!' her hand shook as she raised the coffee pot. Jackson took it off her. 'Aaaaand, I made croissants!' Edna had not gone to too much trouble. The croissants were little balls of frozen dough waiting to be oven-baked for convenience and catering. Edna opened the oven door, and took the entire supply of the Bove's croissants out and rolled them on to the kitchen counter. 'Oops! I forgot to wear oven gloves,' she said.

'Oh dear, quick run your hands under the cold tap for five minutes,' said Diane.

'This coffee's cold!' said Jackson.

'Shh...' Diane quipped.

'I know, sorry I've been waiting aaaaages for you two to wake up...' Edna said. 'I need you to help me break open Genevieve's metal cash box!'

Diane and Jackson looked at one another; they ducked down behind the kitchen counter, collecting several stray croissants from the floor.

'I think she's in shock!' Diane whispered, and Jackson returned her sentiment with an expression of despair.

'Oh, don't worry,' Edna started laughing an uncontrollable laugh. 'She has no money for me to steal, but all her documentations and so on are in there. She's had it years, I should know I've known her years, whoever she is!' more laughter.

'Well, is there no key to this little box?' said Jackson.

'What do you think I've been looking for all night!' cackled unhinged Edna.

'Well, you go and fetch your toolbox, Jackson, and Edna and myself will sit down with fresh cups of coffee,' Diane observed Edna nodding wildly. 'Or maybe we should have tea, chamomile tea perhaps.'

Meanwhile, on Curmudgeon Avenue, love was in the process of being rekindled, and upon hearing about this, Ricky Ricketts was full of regret.

'So you've been FaceTiming the dog all this time?' said Ricky.

'Aww, that's beautiful that is,' Harry the Bastard spoke without moving his eyes from the skirting he was glossing.

'Yes, I would like to think that Shelley the cocker spaniel brought us back together,' said Matteo. Ricky and Harry smirked at one another. They were dying to tell Matteo that they thought he was camming a porn star inside his office with all the noise he was making. Harry the Bastard shook his head at Ricky; although a bromance had developed between the three, they did not want to push it.

'Francesca and me agreed that I could see Shelley on the Furbo camera thingy when she was out at work; she's such a good dog. I could throw treats at her because of the special camera.'

'What happened when you split with Francesca then?' Bored of pet talk, Ricky really wanted to know what had gone on, having gone through a break up himself recently.

'Oh, it's a long story, and I do want us to get finished with this painting today,' said Matteo. The other two males took this as a direction to shut up. After all, men do not talk about things such as these. Silence fell on Number Three Curmudgeon Avenue for what could only have been a matter of minutes. Matteo put down his paintbrush and said to the other two, 'Pub lunch?'

After the briefest of disagreements about which pub was nearer walking distance, the Golden Gate or the Frigate. A decision was made, and all three were treated by Matteo to pub grub and a few pints. They also got to know the low down on Francesca and Matteo's break. It was nothing as salacious as Ricky Ricketts' one-night affair with Gemma Hampsons (resulting in pregnancy). Matteo explained that he had always been a bit funny about commitment, but this was not his fault. His adopted mother, Genevieve Dubois, had no official documents for him. No birth certificate, no adoption certificate, nothing. He had grown up not knowing who he was or where he had come from. His mother had never wanted to talk about it. But the issue came up again when Francesca gave him an ultimatum about marriage. Still, he couldn't marry her because he couldn't prove who he was. So, in turn, he gave his mother a warning and threatened to take her to court if she continued to refuse to tell him the truth. When it came down to it, Matteo could not sue his mother. Genevieve had given him a nominal sum to smooth over the cracks. Francesca was not happy about him falling out with Genevieve. (He did not mention here that she had told Edna she had to borrow a lot of money to pay him off, Matteo didn't know this bit, mainly because it was Genevieve's lie).

'Francesca was happy with being engaged for a bit... Well, ten years actually, but when I eventually told her about the money Mum had given me, she said she would leave me unless I gave it back.' Matteo said. The two other men had lost him by now (told you it was a long story). 'I don't know why I didn't tell her about it in the first place; it wasn't even that much.'

'Oh, I reckon you've got a well good chance of getting her back. It's not like you cheated on her,' said Harry.

'Oi!' said Ricky.

'Numbnuts here can't even remember impregnating his new missus!' said Harry. Ricky Ricketts was welling up with sadness over his actions; he had lost the love of his life, Wantha Rose.

'Well, at least I get to be a dad soon,' said Ricky, lost in his own train of thought.

'The other thing is, Wantha had that photo of your mum on Instagram...'

Ricky kicked Harry the Bastard under the table; he was not present at Tiffin, don't forget.

'You mean a photo of Joanna Lumley?' said Matteo. 'Alright, I admit, it did look like my mother, and after all the lies she told me... who knows?' the three men sighed, not wanting this pub lunch to end.

Back in France,

'And that does it!' Jackson prized open the tin money box with surprising ease. Edna had been correct; there was no money inside. She began rifling through the paper contents.

'Just as I thought,' she said, unfolding a birth certificate. 'Kathleen Henshaw, Date of birth 1950 something, place of birth, Salford. She wasn't even French!' laughed Edna, but this time, her laughter was not caffeine fuelled.

'What!' Jackson and Diane both said in unison. Diane took the paper from Edna's hands. 'Well, hang on, how do you know that this is... well, how do you know this is Genevieve's?'

'Because that's why I really came back. I saw another one of those wanted posters in Paris,' Edna showed them the photo on her phone. 'See, Kathleen Henshaw, not Genevieve Dubois.'

'And not Joanna Lumley either,' said Jackson.

CHAPTER 35: A DÉNOUEMENT

Mr and Mrs Bove went above and beyond what was expected of them as bed and breakfast owners. This is hardly surprising because the Chateau le Grincheaux is above and beyond a bed and breakfast establishment. They escorted Edna through the official channels, surrendering the contents of Genevieve's security tin to the gendarmerie. The Instagram post was also shown, accompanied by lots of pointing and talking loudly and slowly by Edna. The gendarmerie was very interested in the contents of Genevieve's tin. They made hushing gestures amongst themselves, French mumbling occurred, a slap on the back and a handshake was even witnessed. Jackson had to sign something to verify that the person he identified as Madame Genevieve Dubois was, in fact, really called Kathleen Henshaw. Jackson had hesitated at first, as this was all official. Edna had piped up that she was willing to sign, but, embarrassed by her loudness, Jackson gently pushed her aside and fumbled his signature. What did he think was going to happen?

Then came the problem of who was Genevieve's next of kin? Edna thought it should be her, but the authorities thought it should be her adopted son, especially because of all the problems with names. Had anyone any way of getting hold of Matteo Dubois? Edna was asked. No, she had replied. Then she remembered a conversation she had in a private message with Wantha during her return from Paris.

'Oui!' Edna started screeching and trying to grab her phone back.

'Non-Madame!' the policeman said. He started scrolling through Edna's phone, looking for Matteo's phone number. Edna tried to explain that she didn't have it but could get in touch with Wantha via social media. This was all lost in translation. Again, names were the problem. The name 'Wantha' had never been heard in France or any other place in the world, apart from Whitefield. Eventually, Edna sent a message to Wantha, begging her to ask Matteo to contact her. There was lots of too-ing and fro-ing. Wantha got the truth out of Edna and went straight round to Curmudgeon Avenue. Do not worry, this was the day after pub lunch day, so Matteo was at home, and of course, he was not alone. Naturally, Wantha visited Number One. First, Edith was shocked to hear about Genevieve (or whoever she was) passing. And then, Wantha, without her armoury of Spanx and makeup, burst into Number Three Curmudgeon Avenue next door.

'Wantha,' said Ricky Ricketts, observing the love of his life, autumn sun shining behind her voluptuous figure, and through her afro hair.

'Alright, Ricky Ricketts, I need to speak to your boss innit,' said Wantha, staring seductively into Ricky Ricketts' eyes. And in that brief exchange, Ricky knew, they both knew that *'Operation Wantha and Ricky'* had begun.

Matteo Dubois was located in his office, currently Skyping Shelley, the cocker spaniel, but this time, Francesca was also on the other side of the screen. 'Hello, Wantha,' Matteo smiled.

'Lissen, I've got some bad news for you. Edna didn't know how to get hold of you,' Wantha said. Matteo's face fell, and even Shelley picked up on this, moving her head from side to side. Then Harold appeared behind Wantha, interfering in his slippers.

'Edna's on the landline next door; you need to take this call, Matteo,' he said and then continued with mutterings about needing a new house phone for quite some time.

For the following week or so, Curmudgeon Avenue was the colour of sorrow.

Having no passport, or means of acquiring such an official document, Matteo was unable to travel over to France. There is a long and convoluted formal procedure that Matteo could have gone through here. Maybe one day, he will get round to it. For now, he is a nobody. A nobody who paid for his adopted mother's body to be repatriated to the UK. After all, according to the bits of paper Edna found, Genevieve Dubois was really the British Kathleen Henshaw from Salford. Then, of course, there was the funeral to arrange. Would she want to be cremated or buried? Matteo had not seen his mother for ten years, and Edna, it turned out, hardly knew her. Matteo, ever the businessman advertised in the Manchester Evening News, searching for relatives, friends or otherwise acquaintances. No one came forward to claim Genevieve as their own. Kathleen Henshaw, like her adopted son, was a nobody.

The evening before Edna was due to depart from Chateau le Grincheaux, the three bereft friends were alerted to a news report by a face staring from out of the screen. Not Joanna Lumley, but Kathleen Henshaw, the woman, formerly known as Genevieve Dubois. The news report was in French, but they got the gist. Photographs of three males flashed onto the screen; the French poodle even got a mention. A mystery had been born on the Bordeaux border. The body of a woman had been recovered by the authorities from Chateau le Grincheaux, where it is believed she was staying under the alias 'Madame Genevieve Dubois'. A photo of the chateau flashed up onto the screen, causing Jackson mild chest pain. (Fear not, Mr Bove, there is no such thing as bad publicity).

Kathleen Henshaw was believed to be residing at the chateau with her transvestite partner, name unknown. Edna's photo, taken without her consent, flashed up onto the screen at this point; she did not look good. It was from the caffeine-induced day at the commissariat when they handed over Genevieve's documents. Fortunately, Edna had not translated the news report's full meaning, that the story had her down as a man dressed as a woman. Genevieve had been linked to the deaths of three men across France, latterly Eric L'heureux, a foie gras specialist from the Rocamadour area. The police suspected her circumstantially on the grounds of financial motive. However, it now emerged that she had received no monetary gains from any of the deaths.

Furthermore, the sister of victim number two had come forward to say that her brother died of natural causes. He was highly allergic to dogs. Despite French poodles having a reputation of being hypoallergenic, he died of asphyxiation. Police are now searching for animal activists in the case of Eric's death (foie gras is particularly unpopular in this respect). The first death, however, Monsieur Homais, remains a mystery. As the news report ended, Mr and Mrs Bove blew out exasperated gasps in tandem. Edna dabbed her eyes.

'Those poor men.' Edna said nothing else; the facts were staring her in the face, Genevieve, or Kathleen, or whoever she was may or may not have killed these males. Still, the point was, these men had been here, in France, enjoying relations with the woman that Edna loved. (Whoever she was), while Edna was living in poverty in Manchester with her stupid sister.

The following morning, the French sky was full of vapour trails. Edna wished she didn't have to drive her old Ford Cortina back to Curmudgeon Avenue, but the sooner she set off, the sooner she would be back. Besides, there was poppycock talk of bricking up the Channel Tunnel because of Brexit. Speaking of which…

'Thank you for everything you've done,' Edna hugged Mr and Mrs Bove in turn. 'Oh, by the way, I meant to tell you, I think you may have something living behind that portrait of Madame du Pompadour in your guest bedroom. There has been a sound of something moving around all the time we… I've been here!' Edna blew kisses and waved to the Bove's as she departed all the way down their gravel path.

I think we all know that the spy hole in Chateau le Grincheaux is totally getting blocked up.

CHAPTER 36: EDNA'S RETURN TO CURMUDGEON AVENUE.

On a wet Thursday tea-time, the brass door knocker rattled at Number One Curmudgeon Avenue.

'Oh, Edna! Oh, you don't need to knock on the door!' said Edith as she scooped her sister into an embrace. Edna looked down on Edith, trying to put her head close to hers.

'Oh Edith, she wasn't even French!' Edna cried in the vestibule of heartache.

Genevieve's funeral was on Friday, and the wake was at The Frigate.

'So, she wasn't even French then?' said Gil.

'Judge not, Gil Von Black,' started Patchouli, the voice of reason. 'You never got to meet her, did you? That woman was as French as they come. I remember her from the 1980s. She was the most sophisticated thing that Whitefield had to offer at the time. Even if she did have Edna following her, with her big bones,' Patchouli supped a few swigs of her cider.

'The 80s are a bit of a blur to me,' said Gil.

'And the 90s, I expect?' said Patchouli, clinking glasses with her rock star lover.

As so often it happens at funerals, every person had a story about the deceased. Seemingly, everyone thought they had something about Genevieve to tell Edna.

'It's really starting to get on my nerves how everyone else seems to think they always knew she wasn't even French,' said Edna to Edith. Her top lip curled around her teeth, lipstick bleeding into her wrinkles, the same lipstick that left marks on her teeth. For once, Edith was speechless; she had no idea about Genevieve's nationality or otherwise.

'You know, I'm sure I once saw her reading a French phrasebook,' Harold said as he sat down next to Edna.

'Harold,' said Edna.

'Yes?' said Harold.

'Shut it!' Edna gathered her long black dress and removed herself from Radcliffe's very own know-it-all. She went outside, where she met Toonan and Wantha. She reached out her hand into a gesture the Whitefield sisters recognised.

'Sorry Edna, we've only got e-cigs now. Want a drag?' said Wantha offering her vanilla flavoured tube towards Edna.

'We're vaping out here so that Wantha doesn't have to sit in there with Ricky Ricketts and his pregnant sow,' said Toonan, sucking in extra long vanilla steam.

'Oh, that's a coincidence. I've come outside so that I don't have to sit with Harold,' shrugged Edna.

'No...' Toonan shook her head. 'This is not right; this was your girlfriend's wake, let's take it back,' Toonan put on her most powerful posture. 'Come on, Small Paul, we're taking back Genevieve's wake, for Edna!' (Bet you didn't realise Small Paul from Todmorden was here!)

They all went to sit inside with Matteo and Francesca. Despite having agreed to take their rekindling slowly, Francesca had more or less moved herself and Shelley into Number Three Curmudgeon Avenue after the events of the previous few weeks.

'Hello, young man,' brisked Edna. 'And hello, I don't think I've had the…'

'Aww, this is Francesca, Edna; we met in a lift when I was at my new job,' said Toonan, accepting the pint that Small Paul had just got in.

'You've got a job? A proper one?' Edna whipped her head round to Toonan. 'Yeah, I'm a cleaner now, me and Elsie, my workmate we go round houses, businesses… doing all the cleaning.'

'Toonan saved me. I knew she was a people person when we got caught in the lift together,' Francesca gushed. 'And she even got Matteo and me back together.'

'Back together?'

'Yes, we had been together for years, but I got sick of waiting for him to pop the question…' (Oh dear, Francesca's had a wine.) 'So we split up. But I still let him see the dog.'

'On FaceTime,' said Matteo.

'Oh,' said Edna.

'Look at the state of her, the fat cow,' said Wantha seething a sneaky look at Gemma. 'I've had enough. I'm going outside for another vape. You coming, Sis?'

'No, Small Paul's just got the drinks in, stay here, anyway, she is pregnant, she's supposed to look fat!' Toonan said.

Wantha clicked and made her way towards the door. It was only a matter of moments before Ricky Ricketts followed Wantha outside. And after a few doe-eyed glances, they were snogging each other's faces off... It was true what Wantha had said about Ricky Ricketts; he could not resist a bit of Wantha Rose.

Meanwhile, inside, Edna slipped to the ladies.

'I'll come with you!' said Francesca. There was nothing more important than family to Francesca. Edna had a bit of bladder shyness, but soon the two women were side by side at the hand wash facilities.

'So, Edith tells me that Matteo has proposed to you now?' said Edna.

'Yes,' gushed Francesca showing off her engagement ring.

'Well, there is no need for a long engagement,' Edna pursed her lips.

'Oh, we'll have to save up.'

'Save up?' Edna splashed water accidentally on both of them.

'Yes,' embarrassed Francesca. 'Well, I don't want too much of a big do, but, you know.'

'Well, what did Matteo do with all that money his mother gave him? It was only ten years ago, but... don't tell me he has squandered all of it, did he put it towards buying his house?'

'What money?' said Francesca.

'£300,000! Genevieve didn't have that kind of money. I had to remortgage my bungalow. He took her to court!' squawked Edna.

'I don't think so. It wasn't *that* much, even so when I found out Matcheur had taken money from his own mother, I asked him to give it back,' said Francesca. She had absolutely no reason to lie to Edna... Edna, who really was about to reclaim Genevieve's funeral. Drunk Edna made her way to the little dance floor and started fiddling about with the karaoke microphone.

'Hello everyone,' she said. 'I have written a poem about our dearly departed Genevieve. I would so like it if you all listened.'

There was lots of clearing throats and shushing from the wake, except for the heavily pregnant Gemma. She had started fiddling about on her chair in discomfort. The poem was obviously not designed for public consumption. Edna had written it in anger when she found out that Genevieve had lied to her all that time about being French. Now that Francesca confirmed that Edna had been swindled out of £300,000 by the same charlatan, Edna didn't care who heard her bitchy piece of creative writing.

Edna took a swig from her already empty wine glass - embarrassing when something like that happens and unfortunate when the entire pub's eyes are on you. Nevertheless, Edna cleared her throat and began to read:

'*Le Jardin de public*' Edna even put on a French accent for this.

'*When I first met you, you said you were French*

Rescued from Salford, is that what you meant?' (People were looking at one another with puzzlement).

'*The nunnery gave you a fancy new name*

Speaking the language became a game.' (Not strictly true, Edna, Genevieve gave herself that name).

'*Making a life for yourself, and your ways.*' (More shuffling and now groaning from Gemma could be heard over the top of Edna's heartfelt poetic tribute to Genevieve).

'*A picnic of croissant, champagne, sunny days*' (Edna continued despite the racket Gemma Hampsons was making).

'*A long life in the park, le Jardin de public*

I will never forget you, my Madame, my heart'.

The heartbroken Edna retired from her podium to resounding applause from the wake attendees; the poem's hidden meaning was lost to them. And a water-broken Gemma clutched on to the offered arm of Harry the Bastard.

'Does anyone know where Ricky is? I think his

missus has gone into labour!' Harry shouted.

Gemma clutched her swollen middle, and Ricky, with his face smothered in Wantha's lipgloss, re-entered the pub. Wantha, not far behind him, gave Gemma a silent look of triumph and clicked her tongue to the roof of her mouth.

Patchouli and Gil Von Black sat at the same table they had occupied all afternoon. 'Pardon?' Gil said to Patchouli.

'Oh, sorry, I just thought I saw Genevieve standing next to Edna, I was calling her over, but then I remembered she can't hear me. She's dead...'

CHAPTER 37: IT'S A BABY!

Classic cars such as Edith's father's purple Morris Marina are ill-equipped to deal with situations such as their son's pregnant girlfriend going into labour during a funeral. It was a struggle, but eventually, Gemma and Ricky were transported to North Manchester General Hospital's maternity ward.

'You should've just phoned an ambulance,' the midwife said before looking up at the double doors of the ward. Here, what appeared to be the entire congregation of Genevieve's funeral burst in.   'I'm sorry, just father of the baby and direct relatives, please,' the midwife grabbed hold of the wheelchair handles and pushed Gemma Hampsons to the labour ward.

Genevieve's funeral looked at one another. Harold certainly had no place there, perhaps Edith... But Edna, Toonan and definitely not Wantha should be present. Patchouli and Gil Von Black already knew their presence was superfluous. Harry the Bastard had already legged it, putting his amniotic fluid soaked trainers in the washing machine. Like an anxious boy, Ricky Ricketts now wished he had done a runner too.

The birth of a baby can often bring out the best in a person. Wantha Rose did something unexpected; she grabbed hold of Ricky's hands...

'You're going to have to go in there. It'll be alright,' Wantha said.

Ricky looked at Wantha. The midwife looked exasperated. She held the door open, and he disappeared amid screams of his own name; 'RICKY!'

Toonan screwed her mouth into a shrivelled plum shape.

'Pub then?' said Small Paul, who was turning out to be a man of few words; very good words.

Back at The Frigate, there was much pacing up and down in anticipation of news regarding Gemma Hampsons' delivery.

Meanwhile, back at the maternity department of North Manchester General Hospital, Ricky Ricketts treated himself to cheese and onion crisps from a vending machine. He opened the bag with the same amount of noise expected of any crisp packet. But to Gemma Hampsons, the crisp packet being ripped open between contractions was very loud and very annoying.

'RICKY!' she screamed. 'Shut the fuck up!' (Gemma, I did NOT expect this kind of language from a journalist).

'I didn't say anyfin!' Ricky said. Gemma Hampsons was only one hour into her labour. She had ages to go yet, but things can get very irritating in this situation, especially the likes of Ricky Ricketts' presence. Fortunately for him, and straight from the tills at Lidl, Irene Hampsons, Gemma's mother, rushed through the double doors. Harold and Edith pointed to the labour ward, and she rushed even quicker to her side. There were several protestations here, from paternal grandmother Edith and Ricky to the midwife.

'Baby is early and might need an incubator.'

Only to be met by one raised eyebrow from the midwife. Holding a medical chart in her hands belonging to Gemma Hampsons, the full-term mother. (Actually, one week overdue, but let's not split hairs on Hampsons junior's birthday).

'I've brought you a share bag of cheese and onion crisps; I know they're your favourite,' Irene hopefully turned to her daughter. Well, if looks could kill, Irene would be fighting for her life in the neighbouring accident and emergency department.

'I. HAVE. GOT. FUCKING. HEARTBURN!' shouted Gemma. Edith left the room again at this point.

'Well, I'm sorr-ee I thought you wanted me here. Hiya Ricky, love. Oh, I see you've already tried her with the cheese and onion crisps,' Irene said. Ricky was stunned into silence in the corner. 'Ooooh, hang on, you know what they say about heartburn...' Irene was really into the grandmother during labour thing. Neither Gemma nor Ricky had answered her, but she continued. 'It means baby will have hair on its head!' she excited. Gemma threw up everywhere, all over herself, all over her mother. 'A full head of hair by all accounts,' Irene said.

Ricky escaped to have a word with his mother and Harold.

'You might as well go home,' Ricky said. Harold got up immediately and started fumbling in his pockets for the car key. 'I don't know how long she's... I mean baby is gonna to take.'

'Sit down, Harold,' said Edith. 'This is my first grandchild,' her face unsure of the situation, she remembered how her own parents had been when she had given birth to Ricky Ricketts. They were both weeping and promising that their first grandchild (turned out to be their only grandchild) would be their little prince. And so he was... a spoilt brat! With the recent changes in her son's romantic life and Wantha's phantom pregnancy, Edith struggled to be excited.

'I don't know what to do, Mum!' Ricky blurted out. Harold really was desperate to find those car keys now.

'What do you mean? You just be by her side until the baby has come. Then, well, do whatever she tells you to and try not to go crazy when you aren't getting any sleep.' Edith's face had contorted into nervous, toothy desperation. Ricky Ricketts had asked his mother for money many times, but he had never asked her advice.

'No stupid,' Ricky said as though Edith was a mind reader. Harold's ears pricked up. 'Sorry,' Ricky held his face in his hands. 'I think me and Wantha are getting back together...' Ricky peeled his fingers off his face and was met by two pairs of watery eyes. Harold's stuck to his own spectacles, Edith's lips glued to her grinning teeth. All three wondering who was going to speak first. But it was too late for words because the labour ward doors flung open.

'Where the blasted blazes is that bastard midwife?!' shouted Irene. 'The baby's here! It just slipped out of her like the last blob out of a hair conditioner bottle!... Shiiiiit!' Irene ran back into the room, followed by Edith and Ricky. Harold didn't want to look and opted to find the midwife, who was already there and pushed Harold out of the way. Now it was Gemma's turn to wear the face of uncertainty as the midwife took over,

'It's a girl! 10lb 10!' she said, then cradled the baby in a birthing sheet and put her on Gemma's breast.

'See, I told you loads of hair,' said Irene.

'Oh, it's dark, isn't it, lots of dark hair,' Edith and Irene cuddled up to one another, Grandmother bonding. 'She's a bit of a whopper for an early one! I wonder who he takes after?!'

CHAPTER 38: THINGS RETURN TO 'NORMAL' ON CURMUDGEON AVENUE.

If you were to ask what the most annoying thing about returning to Whitefield was for Edna, the most nostril-flaring, excruciatingly painful issue was Harold's bowel habits. His not-so-secret secret is that Harold leaves floaters in the toilet. This secret dragged itself from Harold's stomach, around his colon, through small intestines, into his rectum and escaped irregularly from Harold's unmentionables.

He had to have some pleasures.

Harold would never be honest about when he first started obsessing about his bowels. If asked (and he would not be asked because he would never let it be known), Harold would say he first began to take notice when he was middle-aged. This was about sixty in Harold years. But he would be lying. Harold's bowels had been through a lot during his life, like when he soiled himself in primary school. He seemed to put himself through a lot of stressful and pressurised situations. Black pudding throwing contests, getting arrested, accidentally proposing to Edith at a pub quiz, fighting with a pheasant. His working life, traipsing the streets as a door to door salesman... Or when he was a driver for the zoo, not knowing where his next toilet break would come from. Anxiety and irritation are no good for the bowels. Harold should have thought way back earlier than that, his school days. The shame he brought on his mother when she was handed a little bag containing little Harold's soiled underwear in a Radcliffe school playground. Childhood memories that Harold had banished from his mind. It was little wonder that Harold's digestive system took its revenge in his later years. He was now in the vicious cycle of constipation.

The more Harold thought about it, the more blocked up he became. He had tried various coping mechanisms, castor oil, prunes, and so on. He was a man obsessed and had been keeping a ledger of his motions for the past few years. This included two columns of credit and debits. An intake and export balance chart, if you will. Illustrated, should his doctor ever want to see it. Of course, this put a great deal of strain (!) on the bathroom in Number One Curmudgeon Avenue. Harold could be there for hours; he was in there right now with the door locked. Edith stood outside with her legs crossed, conducting the argument through the bathroom door.

'I wish you would give me a warning when you are going to occupy the bathroom, Harold!'

Just then, on this day that had looked like rain all morning, the heavens opened. The cloud's burst, pelting down and rattling on the up and over garage door. Because of the sound of water, Edith was wet through, right to her knickers (not really). She was scared of having an accident... Edith gathered all her strength together and banged so furiously on the bathroom door that Harold had to give in and vacate the only toilet in the house. Harold grumbled out of the bathroom, and Edith made a dash for it.

'Hey, you! Get to the back of the queue, Harold!' Edna defended her position, also hanging around on the landing, waiting to use the facilities. Inside the bathroom, Edith sat down on the toilet. Oh, the relief! The seat was warm but not in a good way. She could hear Harold and Edna bickering outside about who was next in the queue. I'd better be quick, she thought.

She had just enough time to glance around the bathroom. Harold had made himself quite comfortable there; leaving in a hurry had revealed secrets of his own. A book called *'The Ultimate Guide to Coping With Fools'*... Baby wipes! Well, they are bad for the sewerage... A notebook and pen? Edna was now shouting through the door that she was bursting. Edith turned around to flush the toilet. There it was, one of Harold's floaters. Edith flushed and held her breath until she was out of the bathroom and partway down the landing. Then it was Edna's turn, and what did she see in the bathroom? The same artefacts as Edith, but she also noticed pile cream, a hand-held mirror, tweezers? Liquorice? Uh, no wonder it takes him so bloody long. Add a bit of air freshener to your toilet list, will you, Harold!

Harold and Edith did not speak to each other again that day until it was absolutely necessary. There was a knock on the front door. They looked at each other in horror. They certainly were not expecting anyone. Not at this time (4.30pm).

'Oh, I bet it's one of those door to door salesmen. Or worse, door to door charity hawkers, preying on the elderly and vulnerable in this area. Don't worry, Edith, I'll see them off. You leave it to Harold. They come round here saying, *don't worry, I'm not selling anything!* I say to them, well! What have you come round for then? A bloody chat?' Harold had been going on with himself for so long that the person knocked again. A little voice made its way in through the letterbox

'Hello, Harold? It's me, Mrs Ali. I just want to ask have you had any problems with your drains?'

Edith looked at Harold in horror. He was making his way down the hallway. Mrs Ali, twice as nice but twice as nosy, had been volunteered by the other neighbours to approach Harold about the drain problem.

'Have you noticed any problems with the drains?' Mrs Ali said. 'The drains are blocked, and I think we need to ring the council, darling.'

'Well, that's got nothing to do with us! We haven't got a drain!' Harold said defiantly. Mrs Ali was instantly annoyed at Harold. Stupid man! Where does he think it goes when he flushes the toilet?!

'You don't need a manhole cover in your back yard, darling; they're all connected, they're blocked.'

'Ooo, you know I thought I could smell something,' Edith said. 'I would offer to ring, but last time I phoned the council, they said they couldn't hear me.'

Well, Mrs Ali did telephone the council, and soon, a work van from the water board was blocking the Avenue. The manhole in Mrs Ali's back yard was lifted up, and a corrugated plastic tube was fed down the hole. A crowd gathered. Gossip was rife about the cause of the blockage. Harold sniffed, swallowed, wobbled his head, and tried to listen to the official opinion on the cause of the problem.

'It's usually something simple, something that shouldn't have been flushed down the toilet,' the man from the water board said.

'I read in the newspaper that someone once flushed a human hand down the toilet,' said the wife of the couple who backed on to Mrs Ali's corner shop.

'No, I think that was one of the crime thrillers you've been reading, give you nightmares,' said her husband. A young mother pushing a pram from the house next door, but one joined the crowd. Harold looked at her with his goggle eyes. He leant down and whispered in Edith's ear.

'I wouldn't be surprised if we found a nappy at the end of that tube.'

'Don't be ridiculous, Harold; it'd never get down the U-bend,' Edith said. The woman knew they were talking about her and left the crowd. The stupid old fool, who does he think he is!

'These sewer pipes are an intricate set of equipment, a bit like a maze. They're old though, and sometimes they get constipated,' said the man from the water board. He unconsciously glanced at Harold when he said the word 'constipated'. Now all eyes were on Harold.

'So what you're saying is, the drains are blocked because they're constipated?' Edna chipped in smugly, glancing briefly at the water board man and then glaring directly at Harold. Constipation... Harold knew exactly how the drains felt. Carrying around yesterday's rubbish, blocked up, and taking a long time to clear. He looked wistfully into the manhole. When he looked up again, all eyes were still looking in Harold's direction.

Meanwhile, inside Number Three, and on a break from delicatessen duties, Ricky Ricketts sat on a garden chair in the staff quarters. Wantha Rose sat on his knee. They took a breather from canoodling.

'That baby is more likely to be related to me than you,' said Wantha. 'Have you seen its curly black hair?'

'I know. I just don't know how to break it to her,' said Ricky. Wantha clicked her tongue against the roof of her mouth. They were about to start snogging again, but their attention was drawn to the flashing yellow lights of the utility vehicle and the unmistakable moaning sound of Harold.

'YES! I'm bloody constipated! Alright! Are you happy now?' Harold sniffed, swallowed and gave away his not so secret-secret. He turned on his heel and came face to face with what the crowd was really staring at, at his shoulder level. The connected manhole had blown its own cover. The man from the water board had pressed the sluice button rather than the suction button. The sewer contents were catapulted, projectile fashion, into the sky and all over Harold.

CHAPTER 39: A WELL FANCY DELI.

It was less than two weeks since Baby Emma Fidelity had entered the world (poor little mite). Gemma Hampsons, although refusing to attach Ricky's surname to the tot, had misguidedly attempted endearment with Edith by naming the child Emma. If you remember, this name was the name of Edith and Edna's mother.

Now, I would not say... I would never say that the sisters were glad to see the back of their narcissistic mother... But Edith was relieved that baby Emma had not been born on Halloween – as this would recreate that very same unhappy memory. And as for the child's middle name, well, I think we all know what you're playing at... don't we, Gemma Hampsons?

Emma-Fidelity Hampsons arrival had proved rather challenging for Gemma and Ricky. Her nappies stunk of shit (what else?) And she had the habit of inducing a high pitched and lengthy squeal every time Ricky Ricketts entered the room. Her eyes wide, with that 'baby surprise' face and big *brown* eyes had freaked Ricky out. So much so that Gemma had now banned him from her bedroom. Don't forget, Ricky Ricketts' night of passion with Gemma Hampsons was a distant memory. In actual fact, he could not even remember it. Then, of course, there had been Gemma's '*no sex during pregnancy*' rule... Banished from Gemma's boudoir, it was time for Ricky Ricketts to cut his paternity leave short.

'Oh, here he is!' said Harry the Bastard from behind the swanky counter in the almost refurbished delicatessen. Ricky flopped himself down on the fake Barcelona chair that Matteo had installed for waiting customers.

'Don't, I'm shattered, I don't even know what day it is!' said Ricky.

'Or which woman you're sleeping with?' said Harry, who was putting the finishing touches to some over the counter, stainless steel meat hooks.

'Harry! I'm in a right pickle. Gemma has banned me from the bedroom... but even so, even with how busy we are, every single time my phone beeps, she's like, '*who's that?*' Ricky put his head in his hands.

'Interesting...' said Harry the Bastard, expert

in plots and plans. 'Suspicion can be born from guilt, you know.'

'What?!' Ricky released his face from his fingers.

'I mean, if she keeps wondering who's texting you, then that might be because you should be wondering who's texting her!'

'What? Gemma? Nah, she's all maternatied up still. Still in her slouchy pants.' Ricky dismissed the notion that Gemma could be romantically interested in anyone else. 'Besides, she only has eyes for Baby Emma at the moment. Keeps saying *you look just like Daddy, yes you do*' to her. Thing is, Harry, she looks fuck all like me!'

Harry, who was all heart and had loved many, raised his eyebrow, for he was stuck for words.

'HELLOOOO!' Matteo Dubois gushed through the front door of the soon to be opened well fancy delicatessen. 'Ricky, mate! How's it going?'

'Great,' Ricky shrugged. 'I was just wondering if it's alright to cut my paternity leave short?'

Matteo sucked in a load of air, puffed out his cheeks and blew a meaningful breath. He glanced over at Harry the Bastard, who performed the slightest of nods. 'Yeah, I mean yeah, that'd be great actually, first things first, let's have a brew and tell us all about your baby.'

Ricky Ricketts opened his mouth, ready to commence moaning, but Francesca, having come in the back door with Shelley dog, arrived in the shop.

'Ricky! Aww!' she flung her arms around him. Francesca has fit right in at Curmudgeon Avenue; it's hugs all around in Whitefield. 'Aww, when can I visit? I've got a present for Gemma.'

Ricky squirmed in discomfort. 'She's not really accepting visitors at the moment...'

'Oh?' said Francesca.

'Yeah, well, you're mates with Toonan, aren't you? She doesn't want to have anything to do with anyone who has had anything to do with Wantha.'

'Oh...' Francesca's use of the word 'oh' covered all meanings. 'Oh, I mean, well, does that mean you as well?'

'No, as long as I don't have anything to do with Wantha... I'm banned from talking to her...'

'Haw!' Francesca put her hand over her mouth. 'You mean, she's banned you from having anything to do with Wantha? What about working here?'

'Yes, Wantha Rose is banned from our house, including mentioning her, and as far as working here is concerned, Gemma reckons Wantha has no place here.'

'What!' said Matteo. 'In that case, I'm tempted

to give Wantha a job!' (Go, Matteo!)

Ricky shot Matteo a pleading look. A storm was brewing, and poor Baby Emma-Fidelity Hampsons was trapped in the eye of it.

'Never mind all of that, we have an opening party to arrange,' said Matteo, 'but first, we need to decide on a name, and have a sign made up for the front.'

'I thought you'd decided on a name, boss?' said Harry.

'Ahh keep that to yourself, Harry, I only told you because you said you couldn't make it tonight,' Matteo said.

'Why can't you make it tonight? Is it the new series of *Game of Thrones* tonight?' said Ricky.

'*American Horror Story,*' mumbled Harry.

'What about you, Ricky, can you make it to our meal-out-to-decide-a-name meeting?' said Matteo.

'No... I don't think I'm allowed, I'll just do a few hours here, and then I'd better go back.'

'Ha! Well, make sure you don't drive past the Hillock estate on your way home!' Matteo said 'Looks like it's just you and me tonight, Francesca.'

'Ah, well I have invited someone I hope you don't mind,' Francesca played with her hair because that was the best way of getting her own way with Matteo.

CHAPTER 40: INVITED BUT NOT WELCOME.

'Harold and Edith, I can just about cope with, but Edna?' Matteo fastened his tie. He had arranged for himself and Francesca to visit the new Cambodian restaurant in Bury town centre. His plan was to reveal his idea for the deli's name, plus 're-propose' to Francesca, this time with a ring. So you can see, Edna was invited, but not really welcome.

'Aww, I like Edna,' said Francesca (to be fair, she likes everyone). 'Besides, you have a lot in common; you both loved your mother.'

'Hmm,' Matteo disgruntled.

And so the evening commenced. Matteo, Francesca and Edna made their way to Bury in Matteo's well fancy car. Soon, they were seated in anticipation of Cambodian cuisine. It's a good job that the staff are friendly because the atmosphere between the three diners was tense, to say the least.

'So, how long have you been interested in opening a delicatessen?' Edna had to start somewhere because she had something important to share with Matteo.

'Well, I've always ... to be honest, I just wanted to start a business for the future,' Matteo looked at Francesca. 'When I saw the house was for sale that I lived in with ...' he hesitated.

'With your mother,' Francesca corrected.

'Yes, I just wanted it. I was searching for the truth.... but now I guess I'll never know.'

Edna clutched at her handbag; she had a bombshell in there for Matteo and wondered when would be the right time to drop it... before or after spicy-honey-chicken wing starters?

'The shop used to be a tobacconist, probably explains why it's down a side-street. Do you remember it when it was there, Edna?'

'No! Ha! How old do you think I am? Edna dropped her handbag on to her lap; nervously laughing the truth may have to wait until she'd finished her wine. She gulped it down. It was that time during a meal out when the starters had been cleared, and a further drinks order had been taken.

'There's something I brought back with me from France after your mother died. Everything was just so upsetting. I hope you don't ...' Edna struggled for words. Francesca could not cope with all the emotion she reached for Edna's hand.

'Hope I don't what? I know she wasn't really French... Part of me always knew that...' Matteo warmed up to Edna.

'Quite,' said Edna, who had been utterly bewitched by Genevieve's 'French-ness' and struggled with the notion that *'everyone knew she was not really French'.*

'What is it, Edna?' Francesca said as their table was decorated with all kinds of special curry and wine. Edna took another large gulp from her glass and carefully removed Genevieve's security tin from her handbag. Well, what was left of it after the gendarmerie had rifled through. She knew that the official paper inside would probably come as a shock to Matteo – and part of her did not believe what it meant. He unfolded it, and his eyes took in the information. A birth certificate! Matteo was not used to seeing these, having never had one of his own.

Matthew Henshaw, DOB 1970something.

Place of birth, Paris, France.

Mother Kathleen Henshaw.

Edna stared at Matteo, waiting for the penny

to drop.

'Kathleen Henshaw? Wasn't that the name that my... that Genevieve had previously...' Oh dear, this was going to take quite some time. Matteo, it seemed, was in denial about Genevieve. She had been such a liar that he could not believe anything now. 'Why are you showing me this, Edna?'

'Because,' Edna put her hand on his and gave Francesca *'rescue'* eyes 'I think this is your birth certificate. I think Genevieve really was Kathleen Henshaw, and I think she really was your mother... I'm sorry, Matteo, I mean, she had...' Edna lowered her voice. 'She had stretch marks and everything; she always got undressed in the dark... hmm.'

Francesca dropped the prawn she was holding into her chilli dip. Matteo's hand shook as he looked at the birth certificate again. 'So if she was Kathleen Henshaw, and I'm Matthew Henshaw, then why did she pretend that she'd adopted me? It doesn't make sense.'

'I'm so sorry, Matteo,' Edna sighed. 'I don't know, she was very proud. She always revelled should anyone pass comment on how wonderful it was that she adopted you. I guess we'll never know the truth, though.'

Matteo pushed his plate away. This was a lot to take in. He had wanted to know who he was, but this revelation had thrown up a lot more questions. Edna had tried to help, but the truth had made things worse.

'No wonder she didn't tell me,' said Matteo. 'At least I know why... oh, never mind.'

'Tell you what?' said Francesca.

'Well, it's just that I've had a lifetime of people telling me that my name is misspelt. Apparently, there's only one 't' in Matteo,' (that's your only concern, is it?!). Matteo paid the bill without a care. Edna awkwardly got her purse out to offer her share, but Francesca shut her eyes and shook her head.

'At least you can go ahead with your wedding plans now that you have your birth certificate,' said Edna. Oh! The proper proposal! Matteo had been distracted; perhaps now was not the time.

'Oh, Edna, aww,' Francesca gave Edna a friendly embrace. 'I thought we were going to name the deli tonight!'

'Yes, Francesca,' Matteo held her hand. 'I have an idea, how about calling it '*Francesca's*'?' Matteo swelled with pride. Francesca put her hands to her face.

'Oh! Oh, that's lovely, but wait until you hear my idea... how about we call it '*Genevieve's*'' Francesca's excited face fell on blind bewilderment.

Too soon, Francesca, too soon...

CHAPTER 41: BAD NEWS

Part of the daily routine at Curmudgeon Avenue was to scrutinise the news.

News is everywhere. Harold had even been in the local news himself in the past. Ahh, Gemma Hampsons, the local reporter, currently on maternity leave after giving birth to Ricky Ricketts' (alleged) daughter, Emma-Fidelity.

On this particular morning, the breakfast television programme was running a story about how owners look like their dogs. The smiling presenters reported that researchers had studied this and concluded that 80% of dogs look like their owner. They then discussed how this really meant dogs 'resembling' their owners - that they somehow morphed into one another. Harold and Edith were sat watching this over their morning tea and toast. Harold's head was wobbling out of control, and it was only seven forty-five in the morning. Edith grabbed the plate off the table. She knew that look.

'Dogs looking like their owners! This is not bloody news! Where is my posh writing pad, Edith? This is going to *Points of View*!' Harold spat toast everywhere, making extra vacuuming for Edith. 'Of course, you know what they say, don't you, Edith?'

Here it comes, one of Harold's conspiracy theories. 'When *'they'* start putting nonsense like that on the news, it means *'they'* are hiding something.' Harold's eyes

widened and his lips smacked together in a pompous turkey display. 'Mark my words, Edith, next few days ... Summat big'll be revealed. Proper news.'

'It's a good job we didn't adopt that Irish Wolfhound from the animal sanctuary then.' Edith, not one for thinking too deeply about things, had an uncharacteristic epiphany. Right there in the front room. She looked at her extra-large bowl of porridge, and then she looked at Harold. Had the two of them morphed into one another over the years? She visualised launching a spoonful of porridge at him. Harold was nodding now at the TV.

'Shh, shh, this is more like it, proper news.'

It was about seagulls. The seaside birds had been making a nuisance of themselves in seaside towns. Flocks of seagulls were conspiring to attack coastal areas. Tens of people had been attacked on the promenade; ice-cream cones had been swiped out of their hands.

'Aww, Harold, it's like our honeymoon when that seagull made a mess of my blouse!' Edith also remembered that it had been Harold, not the seagull, who swiped her ice-cream. She looked down at her porridge... but carried on eating it anyway.

A bird expert had been called upon as a special guest on the morning news programme. The reason the seagulls were acting this way was because of humans. Mankind had been overfishing the sea for years, and so the seagulls were searching for alternative food sources.

'We've only got ourselves to blame, see,' Harold said, nodding.

Next, came the recipe section. Today's dish would be a fish dish. Not only that, but the regular medical expert had been called upon to hail the importance of a fishy diet.

'Oily fish are very good for you. Everyday complaints such as constipation can be helped by eating a diet rich in fish,' he spoke out of the TV screen.

Harold squirmed in his seat. The other presenter on the news apologised to viewers who might be eating their breakfast, Harold and Edith carried on eating. Edith did not know which way to turn. Being the type of person who takes bad news personally, she felt she was being blamed for the British coastline overfishing. Yet the next story was telling her to eat more fish. Edith's hand was clenched around her nightdress neckline; she nearly stopped concentrating and missed half the weather report. Edith always liked to watch the weather to see what colour the sky would be that day. Bad weather was feared the most by Edith.

Bad news stories appealed to and affected Harold and Edith for many reasons. Like the one about the contents of a woman's makeup bag being dangerous after reaching a certain age. When Edith said that she was actually wearing one of her mother's mascaras, Harold marched her upstairs. He made Edith open her makeup bag, her handbag, and her dressing table. They were all out of date and far too dangerous. He emptied the bathroom cabinet (apart from his pile cream and castor oil) and threw the contents away. Thank goodness Edith had Harold to protect her from modern dangers such as these. Edith did not wear much makeup, but her fair eyelashes made her face look sort of 'bald' until her mascara supply could be replenished.

Of course, the next part of the news programme was a 'makeover' for a woman who hardly wore any makeup. Edith had to watch while the woman was transformed into a polished, painted lady right in front of the nation. Poor Edith, but thank goodness for Harold, saving her from the dangers of her outdated make-up bag.

Edna, the lady of leisure, was the last person to slope downstairs on this particular day. Being a lover of all things dairy, she helped herself to yoghurt from the fridge. Joining the other two watching breakfast TV, Edna was shocked to discover the news that her consumption of milk and milk products was contributing to all kinds of problems. Global warming, cancer, and bovine distress. She decided to send Harold out to the health food shop to purchase some dairy alternatives for her. From then on, Edna would only be eating soy and nut. No mung beans, though, not with her wind problem.

But then the next bit of news started. Firstly, dairy farmers were going bankrupt. The big supermarkets were involved in some sort of price war. Also, not as many people (like Edna) were consuming milk and dairy products like they used to. Edna considered her forthcoming soya fad. She would be to blame. Farmers up and down the country were starving and losing their homes because of the likes of Edna, not eating as much ice-cream.

The news report went on to say that importing milk alternatives was causing a huge carbon footprint problem. In California, there had been major widespread problems with fires. Fires and droughts continuing right up until the autumn months. They really were having the hottest summer on record. Rainfall and suchlike was one of the causes, but as usual, there was some manmade problem adding to the desolation... Almond trees. There it was. Almond trees increased farming in recent years due to the increased demand for dairy alternatives. The nuts can be turned into 'milk'. Farmed in California because of the sun. Almond trees are incredibly thirsty and so only added to the drought. Well, according to this one particular news story.

'Recent increased demand for consumption of almonds? Blimey, Edna! How much are you planning to drink of the stuff?' Harold said... Now, it is wrong to laugh at your own jokes, but on that occasion, Harold made himself chuckle. 'You ought to be ashamed of yourself!'

Edna flared her nostrils, batted away her imbecile brother-in-law but secretly felt guilty for the parched people and trees of California.

It would not be too long before Edna could take the piss out of Harold again. The next news story was about traffic.

'There's a twenty per cent increase in traffic now! It just said it here on the news and an increase in white vans on the road. All delivering parcels and packages to the likes of you, Harold!' said Edna; she knew all about Harold's internet shopping obsession. If it was not the internet, it would be those flimsy catalogues from the Sunday supplements. (Where else do you think Harold gets his constipation emergency first aid kit from?)

'Very well, today I will drive to Bury town centre and buy my shopping in person,' he huffed. The news continued, moving from too many vans on the roads to too many shoppers venturing into town centres.

Black Friday's Thanksgiving tradition had edged its way further back, almost into October.

'Do not go shopping today unless absolutely necessary', the news report boasted.

The breakfast news had not even finished on the television when Harold drove off in Edith's purple Morris Marina. Edith watched a further story about huge spiders being found in people's bathrooms, bedrooms and cellars. Following one of the hottest summers on record, spiders had enjoyed one of the best breeding seasons they had ever seen. Now that it was autumn, spiders had found new places to spin their webs... In the comfort of people's homes. By November, the start of winter, the presenter reported an: '*Arachnid infestation*'. Edith's hands were well and truly clenched around her nightgown collar.

Meanwhile, Harold had now arrived in the town centre. Imagine his surprise when he struggled to find a suitable parking space; had the shops opened early? Harold turned left onto Haymarket Street. He came face to face with what the likes of Harold would describe as a 'swarm' of people hurling themselves into the shops. They appeared desperate. It was as if shopping was going out of fashion. There was screaming and shouting and pushing and looting.

'Be careful around that old man,' said a woman who looked like she had just stepped out of a TV reality show to her friend (who was equally celebrity styled).

'Sorry, ARE YOU OK?'

Harold did not realise she was referring to him. The woman turned to her friend and said through a heavily lip-glossed mouth. 'Aww bless, he reminds me of when I was on nights at that old people's home. He must have lost his way. I think he might be deaf. Come on, just ignore him. I've got to make a dent in this credit card balance; the plastic won't spend itself!'

The two women turned their backs on Harold and toddled off around the undercover shopping centre. Harold was intrigued. They seemed to know what all the fuss was about. He started to follow them. His goggle eyes focused on their two bottoms that were squeezed into two pairs of skin-tight jeans. Seems like wearing clothes that are too tight is back in fashion, I must tell Edith...

Harold thought to himself. Women in high heels can walk surprisingly quickly, and he nearly lost them in the throng. Harold quickened his step, and sure enough, the unmistakable click-clack of heels and bulging flesh spilling over the top of their jeans appeared again in front of him.

'Let's just go in here, then, we need to go for a skinny cappuccino. I need to tell you all about Louise not answering my event request on Facebook, cheeky bitch!' the second friend said.

'Ooo yeah, and I need something to wear for this Saturday. I don't care if Stuart goes mad about me spending money. I am that close to leaving him, you know.' The lip-gloss friend said, holding her thumb and forefinger one inch apart. This is great fun! Harold thought, listening to people's conversations? I must tell Edith she is correct about the benefits of eavesdropping!

Then it happened... The two women, followed by Harold, stepped into a high street unisex clothing chain. It had fluorescent lighting promising to *'make you individual'*. Although it appeared to Harold, it would make you look the same as everyone else. This was where the crowd was at its worst. The two women were lost to him forever. Pushing and shoving, biting and scratching. Harold was unable to move. He felt like he appeared live in a news report. Proper news, that is. Obviously, there were no 'bits and bobs' to interest the likes of Harold in this shop. With a concerted effort to go against the grain, Harold pushed his way out. The Velcro fastenings on his jacket ripped open. His glasses were skew-whiff. The alarms went off when he stepped through the door. It was no place for the likes of Harold. The security beeping went unnoticed due to the sheer amount of chaos and confusion. Harold walked away with one pair of costume jewellery earrings and one headscarf. Both stuck to his Velcro fastened jacket; he did not even have to try! (Fancy not remembering that Edith does not have her ears pierced, though!)

Harold made his getaway from the town centre, leaving the two women in peace to plan their joint divorce parties. He unlocked the car door of OLD 50DG and tried to start the engine with the same key. Today, the purple Morris Marina was not for turning over. Harold tried again.... it was completely dead. Must be the battery, he grumbled to himself.

Meanwhile, on Sunnybank Road, Pauline Foote (who just so happens to live directly opposite Gemma Hampsons and Ricky Ricketts) was on the telephone to her daughter, Georgina Foote.

'Listen to me, young lady. I've just got my new house straight! You can't phone from Northumberland because you want to move home again!' Pauline absentmindedly peeped across the road at Gemma Hampsons' house while speaking to her daughter. 'What's happened to your fancy fella then?'

There was a pause here while Georgina broke down in heartbreak on the other end of the phone. Pauline was not listening though, she noticed Big George coming out of Gemma Hampsons' house, tucking his T-shirt into his jeans. Pauline needed a better vantage point for this, so she hurriedly ended the call with her sorrowful daughter. 'The world does not revolve around you, Georgina Foote!' Pauline Foote slammed the phone down and ran upstairs, although when she got to her bedroom window, there was no sign of life from the house opposite.

Edna and Edith had enjoyed a relatively pleasant day without Harold on Curmudgeon Avenue. No toilet dramas and neither of them had seen any of the predicted house spiders. Harold had been out shopping for longer than was reasonably necessary. Edith had even tried to start a conversation with Edna about having a tin of peas for tea; 'Just like the old days, if Harold doesn't come back.'

Edna was not keen on this, but not to worry, the sorry streak of nothing that was Harold walked through the back door.

'Oh hello, I didn't hear the car or the up-and-over-door,' said Edith.

'I've got some bad news, I'm sorry, Edith,' Harold sat down, removed his spectacles and used his entire hand to wipe the rain off his face. 'The car's dead, Edith. I'm sorry, it wouldn't start in the multi-storey car park, and the garage recovery people just laughed at me when I said it was a classic car.'

'Huh!' Edith cried. 'Dad only got it out to polish it! He never drove it, and now you've killed it! Where is it?'

'They've taken it to the tip,' Harold said. 'I've had to walk home… in the rain, I might add.'

'I don't even get to say goodbye!?' cried Edith.

'What's this all about?' Edna entered the kitchen.

'Harold has broken Dad's car and sent it to the tip,' Edith grassed her husband up to her sister.

'Sent it to the tip?!' Edna flared her nostrils.

'There was really nothing they could do, honest,' said Harold.

'Oh, it's like Mother and Father dying all over again,' said Edith in floods of tears.

'Come on now, Edith, no need for the waterworks,' said Edna.

'Oh, they do say things happen in threes…' Edith worried. 'First Genevieve, then the car, who's going to die next?!'

CHAPTER 42: WINTER

On this particular day in Whitefield, the sky was filled with grey clouds that looked like porridge. Climbing creepers Edith had planted years ago wound around the garden fence, up the path, and around the door handle.

Despite watching several *Gardeners' World* episodes, Harold had neglected to honour his duties and leaves collected dangerously in massive wet piles on the front path.

Despite the length of time that Curmudgeon Avenue has had to endure their sorry set up, the postman and the window cleaner still regularly got Edna and Edith mixed up.

'Saw your wife the other day, Harold. How is she?' Of course, they meant Edna, not Edith. Harold loved pretending he had two women on the go; he had to have some pleasures, after all. Their accumulative age increased by the day, as you know, time at Curmudgeon Avenue moved rather swiftly.

Routine had become necessary for the three. Every day they read the *'Daily Judgement'* newspaper. How many people were on benefits? Who is stealing our jobs? When is Brexit going to end? There was even an article about how avocados are the most popular cause of domestic accidents in the UK. But the story the three enjoyed most of all was, *whose taxes are paying for it?* Harold's goggle eyes darted about under his glasses. He smacked his lips together, and his neck wobbled like a turkey.

'Halloween and bonfire night means winter is here. I am NOT answering the door!' Edith's fingers clenched around the neckline of her nightdress.

'And I am NOT getting deafened this year by whizz-bangers!' Edna asserted. As if *she* could do anything to stop North Manchester's population from setting off fireworks! Harold was already plotting an idea of how to protect his wife and sister-in-law from the perils of winter.

'Don't worry; I am in charge of all things firework and Halloween-y. You leave it to Harold.'

He then launched into a story about why Catherine wheels are called Catherine wheels, getting it very wrong. Proof, by repeated assertion.

Anyway, Harold and Edith went shopping. Edna stayed at home, continuing to read that article in the paper.

INCREASE IN FATAL HOUSEHOLD ACCIDENTS

'They should do something about that,' Edna said to no one in particular.

At the supermarket, Harold found what he was looking for in the '*special buys*'. Noise-cancelling headphones and a trick doorbell, in preparation for noisy fireworks. He popped them into his rucksack. Harold had never been caught shoplifting. People were usually too busy looking at Edith wearing a nightdress under her coat. When they got home, Edith opened the garage door. As you know, this meant she had to lock it from outside, walk down the entry, down the side street, down Curmudgeon Avenue and up the path.... in the rain.

Inside, Harold and Edna took it in turns (Harold first) to try on the headphones for bonfire night. Because they were wearing the headphones, they did not hear Edith's scream as she slipped and skidded on the slippery leaves on the front path. Her skull crashed into the front door with her nightdress over her head. There Edith lay, concussed and freezing to death under a massive pile of wet leaves.

Harold always had his rucksack with him, often forgetting how much space it took up. Edna followed him into their dingy hallway. Harold set about fitting the doorbell. He reached in for the multipurpose screwdriver and smiled to himself when he felt the contents of his rucksack. Spare socks, Breath freshener, and a tin of peaches he was saving for later. The trick doorbell was designed to send a mild shock to whoever buzzed it. *'As seen on celebrity reality TV'* was emblazoned in big letters at the top of the cardboard packaging. Harold lifted his rucksack, swung it around his back and hit Edna clean in the face. The weight of it knocked her to the floor. Harold was still wearing the headphones, so he did not hear the thump. He fitted the doorbell, but the combination of multi-purpose screwdrivers and steamed up spectacles made for a poor job. The electric shock knocked Harold flying backwards on top of his rucksack and on top of Edna. The fancy rucksack straps garrotted him as he fell and smothering any remaining breath from his sister-in-law.

Edna was right; people do die in threes... or was it Edith who said that?

Acknowledgements and stuff.

Samantha Henthorn was born in Bury in 1970something. She is a disabled middle-aged housewife who used to be a nurse but now writes books.

Her stories are all set in the North West of England and are written with British English spelling and grammar. This includes a northern turn-of-phrase, no one ever says 'and I' in Manchester.

Thank you to my friends and family, especially Mr Henthorn, who has provided excellent husband skills. Thank you for reading the Curmudgeon Avenue series. If you liked it, tell all your friends. If you didn't like it, tell no one.

Special thanks go to my beautiful daughter Alicia. When I asked her for Parisian hotel names, she said, 'I don't know, make something up...' So I thought, what would Hotel Daughter sound like in a French accent?

Thank you to Maggie Melville, Neil Warburton and Danny Ward for your proofreading skills. Danny lived in France for a year, but as Genevieve wasn't even French then... meh!

Thank you to Deborah J Miles at Against the Flow Press for reading and reviewing Edna and Genevieve Escape From Curmudgeon Avenue; give this great blog a visit at https://againsttheflowpress.blogspot.com

Thank you to Elizabeth Chadwick and Margaret

Skea for the intertextual references. There is no such thing as bad publicity – and Edna and Genevieve have good taste in literature, thank you.

You are invited and welcome to give me a follow on my blog SamanthaHenthornfindstherightwords.blog

Or sign up for my mailing list https://landing.mailerlite.com/webforms/landing/d0q2h7

An audiobook version of Edna and Genevieve Escape From Curmudgeon Avenue will be released very soon. Produced by the multi-talented voiceover actor Lindsay McKinnon at @LindzMcKinnon (Twitter) Theatre of The Mind Productions TheatreOfTheMindProductions.com.

You may have realised that this is not entirely over; Curmudgeon Avenue is not going to be knocked down just because Harold, Edith and Edna have passed on. Someone has to live there… Patchouli and Gil need to move to America, Small Paul and Toonan are getting serious. What of Wantha Rose and Ricky Ricketts?

The next book in the series is 'The Ghosts of Curmudgeon Avenue' available from Amazon.

MORE BY THE AUTHOR

1962 (An Uplifting Tale of 1960s Lancashire)

Piccalilly (A Remembrance Day Story)

Quirky Tales to Make Your Day (24 short stories)

Curmudgeon Avenue (six part series)

What We Did During Lockdown (An Anthology Written During the Time of Covid 19)